The Book of Squidly Light

Imaginary Author at Large in the Multiverse

*Shifting dimensions, eccentric aliens,
and batty earthlings.
Love, hope, courage, and acceptance—
but there is danger!*

THE SAGE CHRONICLES
by Karima Vargas Bushnell

Welcome to mysterious writer Halycon Sage's Multiverse, where relatively ordinary events open into places of multiple meanings, multiple possibilities, and multiple points of view.

Book One
THE WAY BEYOND

Sage and No-Name Stupid, his TV-watching, motel-sleeping horse, have escaped into the western desert to save the world. They're helped by a brilliant but eccentric Czech inventor, an Iraqi-American family facing ruin, Ruby—resourceful queen of the Dirty Dog Gang—and Ratbone of the Fifth St. Mofos. They're opposed by some detectives, some spies, and a shadowy figure of evil. The book critics, outlaws, and tiny invisible robots could go either way.

Companion Anthology
SAGE'S MULTIVERSE MINI-SERIES

The latest from our imaginary author, an intricately woven tapestry of viewpoints and characters: short stories, mini-novels, poetry, interviews, diaries, and more. Encounter the Green World and the World of Light, Five Tips for Intergalactic Diplomacy, bewildered writer Karima navigating the chaotic world of airports, and a Cat Attorney who shares his diary and advises a canine inquirer on *dogagories*. So jump into a novel, a post or a poem. You never know where you'll come out, but you know it's going to be an awesome ride!

ALA BookList Magazine / BlueInk
Review pick for March 2020
The Book of Squidly Light is Back
In a New Edition that's Squidlier than Ever!

Karima Vargas Bushnell's **The Book of Squidly Light** *is an eclectic, genre-bending novel exploring spiritual messages with tongue-in-cheek comedy.* **—BlueInk Review**

Here, we find [Sage] just where he left off: dwelling in a world recently purged of modern technology and escaping into his writing, unaware of how his words impact a fluctuating multiverse. In a metafictional conceit worthy of a Charlie Kaufman film, it turns out that while Bushnell is the creator of Sage, Sage is the author of Bushnell and the reality—our reality—where she exists. In Sage's world, he's joined by a multicultural cast as they navigate the sudden discovery of a squid-like race of intelligent extraterrestrials. Meanwhile, in his fictional creation (our world), a mad dictator has come into power, threatening everything that really matters.

Setting things right will bring both worlds together in a collision that extends consciousness to inanimate machines, exposes politically motivated time-travel conspiracies, and harnesses the spiritual power of the written word . . . the novel eschews the darkness of dystopia and finds hope in the shadows of apocalypse.

The adventures of a mysterious writer continue in a post-apocalyptic world. **—Kirkus Reviews**

Bushnell's narrative tone is carefree throughout... the plot pinballs among its various subjects with a manic intensity and a surplus of quips and absurdist jokes. This gonzo style is undeniably entertaining on a page-by-page level ("it's something called badinage," one alien tells another. "It's supposed to be funny").

The Book of Squidly Light is a spirited and philosophical science fiction novel whose humor abounds. **—Foreword Reviews**

v

Halycon Sage, a famous writer of very short books, meets aliens, enemies, and fights to stave off nuclear annihilation in Karima Vargas Bushnell's wacky science fiction romp The Book of Squidly Light.

Halycon, whose mind shifts "between worlds and dimensions, reality and fantasy, tragedy and laughter," survived the apocalyptic incident known as The Event. He lives with other survivors in a small town, where he encounters cephalopod-like aliens called Squidren. Interspecies social interactions, romance, nanobots, time travel, an alternate universe, and a cat who's also an attorney factor in thereafter, blurring reality and fiction: the text even involves an "imaginary author," Karima Vargas Bushnell.

Free-wheeling and unpredictable, the story proves to be dynamic . . . Delivering random but inspired humor and social insights, The Book of Squidly Light is a spirited and philosophical science fiction work.

The Complete Works of Halycon Sage

From The Way Beyond

One-Hundred-and-One Cows: A Novel
Everything in the Universe is Fine Right Now
The Crushing Fall and Phoenix-Like Resurgence of
    Halycon Sage: Part Forty-Two of the Chronicle of
    My Life: Stuff I Did, Why I Did It, What It Felt Like,
    and Why You Should Care (unfinished)
And a Man Went Forth
A Man Reading a Book
Boo Radley Goes Hawaiian

From The Book of Squidly Light

Hat!
Stranger
Romance for Cat and Squid
The Forget About It Trilogy; also known as
    *The Dinosaur Trilogy:**
    The Land Before Time Forgot Itself
    The Land the Dinosaurs Forgot
    Forget About It

Meeting Glass: The Poetry of Halycon Sage**

Meeting Glass — Halycon Sage
But Look at China! — The Squidren of Squidship One
Resourceful Horse — No-Name Stupid
Optometrist, Eye Thyself — Fatty Lumpkin
The Patterns, the Patterns! — Karima Vargas Bushnell
Too Many Drugs in Here — Fatty Lumpkin

*See Appendix C
**And friends

The Book of Squidly Light

The Continuing Chronicles of Halycon Sage

Book 2

Karima Vargas Bushnell

*The New Bestseller
That's Sweeping the Dimensions*

The Sage Chronicles

The Book of Squidly Light

by Karima Vargas Bushnell

Published by Delirious Walrus Productions LLC
Minneapolis MN
Second edition May 2024.

Because of the dynamic nature of the internet, any web addresses
or links contained in this book may have changed since
publication and may no longer be valid.

Paperback: 979-8-9903114-5-9
Ebook: 979-8-9903114-9-7

Library of Congress Control Number: 2019948459

Cover Design by Richard Ljoenes LLC

Illustrations and Interior Design by
Faye Howell
B.C. Hatch
And Pankaj Ruthala

Edited by
Delirious Walrus Editing Department,
Rabbi Yonassan Gershom
B.C. Hatch
Chandi Lyn

DEDICATION

**To the incubator babies,
with all my love forever**

THE SPACES IN BETWEEN

Warning: While you may experience this introduction as serious or even stuffy, you should know that there are those who find *The Book of Squidly Light* "absolutely hilarious".

I DON'T EXACTLY write my books. They come to me, first as an energizing, joyful spark, then as a direct, "Okay, you need to write this down." After that I trim and edit and fine-tune, a process which may take hours, days, or years. *The Way Beyond* started that way; I woke one morning hearing the words, "One-Hundred-and-One Cows: A Novel". My protagonist, Halycon Sage, had roughly the same experience.

The human body being what it is, we move right and left, up and down, forward and back. My Squids—or *Squidren*, as these interdimensional space aliens call themselves—can move in any direction: diagonally through air or water; mentally, emotionally, or physically through time and space. The Squidren are a talented species. And though I didn't set out to create them, both the word-obsessed Squidren and the sandwich-making Nanobots seem to have manifested partly because I saw no hope of anything less bizarre and drastic pulling our glorious planet out of its current, human-caused mess.

The winds of history affect things previously written, changing their meaning and holding a magnifying glass to one subject out of many. While I'm tempted to address current global and political issues here, I am resisting that temptation as it would pull the whole thing out of alignment.

The 'Middle East situation', which I no longer find baffling, is highlighted briefly in *The Way Beyond* and also in my play, *Voices on the Waves*, but it is only one of many interrelated subjects these works embrace: identity, absurdity, commercialism, consciousness, society, post-modernity, social justice, space aliens, animals and the earth, communicating across cultures, and many other topics both serious and silly.

The blog which formed the basis for *Sage's Multiverse Mini-Series* posed the questions, "If you're *raised* by a nonconformist to *be* a nonconformist and you conform to that programming, does that make you a conformist?" And "What if your parents were opposites, one violently at odds with the local culture, both hiding or denying at least one identity? What if you never had any coherent culture to conform to even had you wished to?" That was my situation; possibly it was yours as well.

Then there's non-ordinary reality, which informed my worldview since early childhood: unusual in the 1950s global West, but far less so in other parts of the world and in the 60s and 70s cultures where I came of age.

Upon discovering the Intercultural Relations field, I found that people imprinted with two or more cultures, no matter what those cultures are, have a shared perspective: a realization that many things others see as irrefutable truth are, in fact, cultural constructs. What I call the Spaces in Between are the undefined places separating worldviews, the malleable borderlands between ethnic, national, class, economic, religious, and other kinds of cultures where certainties dissolve and there is room to move, to explore, to innovate, and to meet those previously considered "others".

May that freedom, as manifested in this book, be interesting and hilarious and helpful to you, the reader. All of us—The Sage & Squid Editorial Board; the aliens, humans, animals, and Nanobots who live in my head; and my humble or not-so-humble self—wish you the very best.

May the Horse be with you.

There are many things in
The Book of Squidly Light.
The book before you is one of them.

SQUID!

by Halycon Sage

"*BREAKING NEWS!! Alien Time Travel Scandal Spins Out of Control!*" wrote Halycon Sage, celebrated founder of the Post-Modernist Minimalist Neo-Symbolist Pseudo-Realist School of Literature.

"There!" he exclaimed with satisfaction, throwing down his pen. "*That* oughta hold 'em for a while."

"And that's it? Nothing else?" A fine, ruby red brow arched over a strangely-shaped eye, creating an air of polite skepticism.

"What? I have to tell the whole story? Do you realize *how many pages* that's gonna take? And nobody will ever believe it."

"Of course they will," said the off-world visitor soothingly, "if they hear it from *you*."

This is the story he told.

PART ONE

THE DINNER

WHEREIN the Blue Thread is unveiled and illumined.
The Squidren embody the qualities of Blue.

CHAPTER
ONE

Introducing the Green Thread

ut first, we must give a nod in passing to the *Green* Thread. Green for the Earth, you see, and the environment, and what was happening to it, and what Preisczech did about it with the Nanobots, causing what was originally styled "the End of the World!" but later became known simply as the Great Event and finally just the Event.

The sudden disappearance, with some exceptions, of all technology foundational to modern and post-modern civilization—in fact pretty much everything invented since the Industrial Revolution—had been a shock to the citizens of Dry Creek Gulch. Such was their dependence on post-modern technologies that at first they were more distraught by the loss of their cell phones and internet accounts than by the threats to food, water, and shelter. This phase passed quickly as taps yielded their last drops and food began to spoil. Wild rumors abounded, but strangely, most people moved from denial to first attempts at coping without any intervening stage of terror.

Some self-indulgent citizens—shamefully, world-renowned author Halycon Sage was among them—would have curled into small balls beneath their covers and waited for somebody *else* to do something, but Ruby was having none of it. She and a few others were getting the townspeople organized. Though the Event was only weeks in the past and things were trending in a good direction, Ruby wanted everything to move faster.

"You, kid!" she called out an open window. "Get everybody to the Dirty Dog in thirty minutes. Step on it!"

"Step on what?" asked Nuri. He was brilliant, though very young, and did not have a particularly literal mind, but the constant switching between Arabic, Ebonics, and various dialects such as Old Hippie and Preisczech's sprung English had left him ignorant of idioms.

"That means hurry up!" said Ruby, grasping his confusion. And he did.

"Food Committee, Water Committee, Emergency Committee, Foraging, Other Stuff . . ." mumbled Sophie, distributing the large, stiff pieces of cardstock around the main room of the Canis Fidelis Grill and Juice Bar, formerly the Dirty Dog Bar. Brushing back her copper hair, she looked around with satisfaction. Though the committees were new, they had already done some remarkable work. Most notably, Food had discovered a system of caves, part of which was cool enough to act as a refrigerator.

"Pick your spot, ladies and gentlemen, pick your spot," called Ratbone. On the whole, the women were taking the situation more calmly than the men, being generally more practical, but Augustus T. Rathbone (a.k.a. Ratbone) was unaccountably cheerful.

Or perhaps it *was* accountable. Despite his pre-Event identity as the desperado head of the Fifth Street Mofos, he had barely committed a crime in decades. Unaware of the broader context of the world's end, he had been excessively worried by the damage done to the beautiful black limo he'd rented in the run-up to the end times. He was cheered by the realization that he was immune from prosecution regarding the beloved vehicle, which no longer ran—no cars did. Even better, he would never have to return it. It had no worth except as a make-shift greenhouse and there was nowhere to return it to anyway, but somehow this knowledge made his heart happy.

Jenny sat at Food. Preisczech had certainly caught a lucky break from fate: his new wife, who had appeared out of thin air when his need was greatest, was not only sweet and pretty but a monster cook, canner, baker, and pickler, able to do several of these things at once while patiently and clearly instructing others. Good talents to have after the end of the world.

Preisczech took his seat at Water along with Sophie's brother Josh and Josh's friend Trevor—two young men whose incipient genius must henceforth be directed toward the physical rather than the virtual world. Preisczech, like Sophie, was mumbling to himself, "Shelter, Fire, Water, Food. Shelter, Fire, Water, Food." He was not quite sure of the order, and he pronounced the hot element "Fy-yer" so the rhythm, regular till it ended with a bump at Food, would not be disturbed. Preisczech had always had a penchant for these little chants. They soothed him.

Muhammad Abdurraheem Hussein (pronounced Ab-DURE-rah-HEEM), former pilot and misunderstood Iraqi immigrant, sat intrepidly at Emergency. He leaned forward, eyes sparkling with anticipation. *Yes, intrepid, that's what I am, ready for anything. Ready to come back and show what I'm made of!*

From the tone of his thoughts, he had been hanging around too much with Preisczech. He was wondering if it would be possible to build a glider out of scrap metal. A glider could be useful and would not require energy sources that no longer seemed to exist.

"Energy!" cried Sophie, perhaps tuning in to her neighbor's thoughts and quickly making one more label. She *knew* she had forgotten something. So what if combustion engines didn't combust and gasoline and oil unaccountably sat there, refusing even to catch fire under the influence of flint and steel. There was solar, there was wind. Plenty of those, though there was no tidal power to be had in this southwestern desert. But methane . . . maybe something could be done with chicken manure.

Sophie, recent valedictorian, budding intellectual, and amateur book reviewer of discerning literary tastes, had never thought she would be getting excited about chicken manure.

As usual when anything noteworthy happened to him, Halycon Sage wrote it down in the form of a story, speaking of himself in the third person. Now, as in former times when he had been an internationally famous author cloaked in mystery, he did not distinguish between fact and fiction. This was the source of both his genius and his . . . well, not madness exactly, but occasional confusion. So, what follows is what he wrote, or what he experienced, or possibly both.

Something Stupid This Way Comes
What Happened to Halycon Sage
(with apologies to Ray Bradbury)[1]

Halycon Sage was out behind the town dealing with a large brush pile, which might make excellent kindling on the one hand or present an uncontrolled fire danger on the other. He was also thinking. He thought it odd that only one visitor had arrived in town since the end of civilization several weeks ago. A few people had *left*, apparently heading into the mountains, but almost no one had arrived. And while everything was pretty much banjaxed, there were still roads, horses, and bicycles, and the town, though remote, was not *that* remote.

Either Sage was turning psychic with the passing years or good old serendipity was at work, a ridiculous word if there ever was one (though a quick consulting of his pocket dictionary told him that serendipity was supposed to be *fortunate*, so the word might not apply). Because just as he was considering the absence of visitors, he saw a wagon coming up the road. A small, dilapidated, one-horse kind of wagon, like something from the Hollywood wagon trains he'd seen in his youth, but much less impressive. As far as he could see in the fading light, it was being towed by a dark brown mule, and there was no visible driver.

The wagon pulled even with him as he stood unobserved behind the brush pile. He still couldn't see a driver, though there was a shadowy presence in the right general area. He turned his attention to the wagon itself. Squinting, he was able to make out fancy scrollwork letters, painted in bright colors.

Cougar and Dark Pandemonium Shadow Show

"Huh," said Halycon Sage, making the sound generally transcribed by 1950s screenwriters writing Indians as Ugh. "*This* can't be good."

Sage was a reader, even more so since he'd teamed up with Ruby, and he knew what the words implied. Still, nothing in his reading would have signaled the presence within the wagon of the self-styled Apocalypse Zombie.

CHAPTER
TWO

Have patience, Reader.
This is a braid of five strands.
Be patient with the braiding.
This is a braid of five threads: The Red, the Green,
the Yellow, the Blue, and the Black.
Have patience as they are introduced.
They will be braided together at last.
And then you will see.

—*The Book of Lighted Squid*, Volume 24, Canto 115

Introductory Squid Interlude

SQUID TWO: Commander, this two-sentence novel *Hat!* by Halycon Sage is the only example of Earthean post-apocalyptic literature we've been able to find. Together with the two reviews, of course, and some strange additional notes from the author. Surely these things must be taken together as one art piece.

(He lifted the manuscript reverentially on three of his arms. This probable revelation of the unique alien Earth culture, this treasure from the depths of space. Obtained through methods known only to the Squidren.)

SQUID ONE: Well, go back down there and find something else. It's terrible.

SQUID THREE: Excuse me, Commander, I believe it's something called badinage. It's supposed to be funny.

SQUID ONE: Well, it isn't. If we report back with this, they'll have our heads.

SQUID THREE: But Commander, we found it, so it has to go in the report. And before we land, too!

SQUID TWO: We could shove it to the back, direct those interested in badinage to the proper page, and get on with our work.

SQUID ONE: Excellent idea. Do that.

(And they did, marking and bundling the precious novel, the reviews, and the apparently meaningless digressions to the end of their report so future researchers could decipher their hidden meanings. For surely nothing in this text from across the stars could be meaningless. See Appendix B).

Ruby was so busy organizing and planning she had not yet noticed the absence of Halycon Sage at the community meetings. Alone among the prominent citizens, Sage was generally missing from these discussions. He was neither contributing to the group effort as he should have been, nor hiding in an isolated pout, as might have been expected. He was writing.

There was some oppositional quality in him that had been activated. When he was *supposed* to write, because he was a *writer*, he had hated the very idea and done everything he could to avoid it. Now that it was a guilty pleasure, he was working on several projects at once.

At a certain point, a frank discussion could no longer be put off.

"Sage, we've got to talk," said Ruby, coming into the Dog one morning with a purposeful air.

Ruby always called him "Sage," addressing him by his last name as Victorian wives and certain women up to the 1950s had addressed their husbands. (Although they had not yet married, the matter was under discussion.) After all, you couldn't really call anybody "Halycon," not full time, anyway. For a moment she imagined addressing him as "Hal" and shuddered. She would never tell him this fleeting thought.

Sage was peeling apples. Someone had set him this simple task, to do with an incipient pie, and he was quite content with it. "Yes, my dear?"

"My dear," might sound odd from a (probably) Native American in the 21st Century, but various books from England had been read to him as a child, though his amnesia was still pervasive enough that he had no idea where or by whom. Perhaps being mistakenly raised as an East Coast intellectual in the heart of the Nevada desert had something to do with his way of perceiving and code-switching, but his odd turn of mind came in handy with Ruby, who was herself a woman of many aspects.

"You've got to do something," said Ruby flatly.

Sage looked at her quizzically, indicating the apple and paring knife in his hands. Peeling *apples* was doing something.

Ruby, momentarily distracted, thought how she loved his hands, the strong yet delicate brown fingers. She had thought quite a lot about what Sage should be doing in this new world, partly because he didn't seem overly concerned with the matter. She was busy all the time, often organizing, but also lending a hand with even the most physical tasks. Sage, by contrast, seemed to spend a lot of time sitting around daydreaming. He also had a habit of disappearing into the old shed where the clacking Smith Corona typewriter was stored. Ruby suspected he was writing again, and while otherwise delightful, a new Post-Modernist Minimalist Neo-Symbolist Pseudo-Realist novel was not exactly what the present situation required.

Sage should have been good at all physical things. He was strong and well-coordinated, but he had a way of slipping into his own reality at the most inconvenient times, coupled with an occasionally dangerous tendency to trip over his own feet or over the piles of stuff he seemed to find it necessary to take with him everywhere.

She smiled, thinking of the habitual grace and the occasional stumble. She had given up on relationships years ago, finding most men more trouble than they were worth. Yet every man she had really loved, every single one of them, had been someone she could laugh at—not unkindly, but with a kind of releasing joy. That touch of absurdity sealed the deal for her somehow. They had to be just a little ridiculous. She shook herself mentally and refocused.

"I mean something real. A *man's* work."

Sage grimaced. They were both old-fashioned in some ways, and surprisingly, Ruby was sometimes the more traditional of the two. He knew it was pointless to argue.

Over the next few weeks, she tried him on cooking, fishing, making useful things out of wood. At all of these he was reasonably competent, but uninspired.

Something else, thought Ruby, *something else.* Then one fine day, since guns were no longer an option, she took him bow hunting. He was a natural. His shots were so accurate as to be almost painless to his quarry. It was certain he had been carefully trained somewhere, at some time, though the remaining foggy patches in his mind concealed the details.

So, that was settled, and Sage became the town's premier hunter. He mostly went alone, but sometimes took one or two others with him. The quickest, most skilled and accurate, but also the most trouble to keep quiet, was Basel Deadeye Vasselschnauzer, former literary critic and sometime dart-board champion. The man moved like lightning, graceful as a ballet dancer, and his tendency to whine about every little discomfort seemed to be decreasing. It was almost worth it.

Perhaps living nearer the land, testing themselves against concrete problems, was healthier for people than battling vague neuroses and layers of complexity. Given the post-apocalyptic nature of the situation, it was quite surprising how many people were actually having fun.

In one of the dark and shadowy places that can be found even in a sun-washed desert town, a shadowy man was speaking to his emissary.

"There are always problems to be exploited. Unspoken grievances and misunderstandings, little troubles to be rubbed the wrong way, developed into sores. People who feel unacknowledged, people who feel passed over. Work on those."

The shadowy man nodded. "That will be all."

The emissary withdrew.

CHAPTER

THREE

Introducing the Blue Thread

The ship was nearing Earth, reaching the point where the voyagers would have to start considering and dealing with what they were about to face. They did not *want* to, but there was no choice.

"The Earthans . . ." said Five.

"Don't you mean the *Earthe*ans?" interrupted Three. "It flows better."

Even in this extremity, the Squid were prepared to argue about language—not the meaning of it so much, but the music of its internal rhymes and stresses, the singing vowels, and the biting and hissing consonants. This was their approach to *every* language. It was only with great trouble that some bizarre young radicals had convinced them to pay attention to the *meaning* of the aliens' words. They still thought the idea absurd and had persistently transcribed the start of Abraham Lincoln's Gettysburg Address, one of their language exercises, as, "FORCE core rands ebony-EARS saGO," which they thought quite pleasing for an artifact of a primitive race, though obviously something was rhythmically wrong with the "y" in the middle.

"We could call them Earthlings." Seven, a younger and technically inclined Squid, had managed to tap some Earthean entertainment broadcasts.

"That implies that they are little." Four gently entered the conversation. A discussion about words would always pull everybody in, no matter what practical work needed to be done. "Is it not insulting?"

"Perhaps they enjoy being insulted," said Five. "We know so little about them."

"If they are small, they should be called Earth*lettes*," opined Six, a second mate.

"But as the females are known as Earth*ettes*, that would be very confusing," interjected Nine.

"I believe that formation is antiquated," said Four. "And is also insulting."

"These Earthers are certainly easily insulted," said Three. "They seem a touchy lot."

Well, that was obvious. If the Earthers had not been touchy beyond belief, the Squid would not have been there at all.

I wonder what they call their zi-chen, thought Eleven, gliding away to address *zi's*[1] regular duties. Eleven was one of several members of a third gender, or collection of genders, aboard the ship.

While the research results on Earthean males and females had been fairly conclusive, though odd, research on their zi-chen had been far odder and so contradictory, especially when combined with incomprehensible Earthean attitudes toward *color*, that it was decided the Squidish zi-chen should stay on the ship during First Contact. It would not do to appear stranger than necessary to the Earthers in the event that they were radically culturally and biologically different from the Squid.

Interlude: Meet the Apocalypse Zombie

He'd awakened the day after the Event in a fortress-like, cement-filled building that had a huge hole blown in the wall. He sat up in his narrow cot with some interest. He could see out. He could see ground and trees and sky in front of him. This was most unusual. Also unusual was the absolute silence, except for a morning chorus of birds, and the apparent absence of other people, either patients or staff. He shouted experimentally, the kind of crazy yelling that usually brought instant response.

Nothing.

---

1 *Zi (pronounced "zee") is a personal pronoun in Squidish. It is not used for objects, like "it," but for sentient beings whose gender falls beyond or outside a binary gender conception. The term is also used when the gender of a being is unknown or for members of groups with mixed genders.*

He reached for his glasses, and they were reliably there, the only reliable thing, apparently, in this newer and crazier world. You'd think things couldn't *get* any crazier than being locked in a mental institution, but there you go—life is full of surprises. He didn't remember much, though the transition from his college art department to his parents' basement to the loony bin was not the kind of thing people generally forget. Like Halycon Sage, whose works he had studied with awe in his not-so-distant student days, this young man had persistent memory problems, perhaps brought on by stress or by unwise medical decisions. Unlike Sage, he knew his real name, but he had no desire to remember or retain it. His previous life had gone badly enough that he was glad it was over.

He sat still, considering his options. This was obviously a new world, and he would just damned well become a new person to go with it. There was a cracked mirror in the room, and he stepped over to it. His first intuition was confirmed: his appearance was grotesque enough to embody the character he had envisaged. He sighed. *Any identity is better than none*, he supposed. And certainly *someone* needed to do it. He picked up a few belongings and walked out through the hole in the wall.

Finding a small covered wagon with a dark brown mule grazing beside it a few blocks from the mental institution did not really surprise him. He obviously needed some form of transport and here it was. The abandoned cars he had found with keys in them did not work.

Near the wagon was a small bale of hay, and he heaved it on board in case he ended up in the desert. The addition of several colorful paint cans, an empty bucket, and an assortment of brushes on a wooden platform nearby was just pure gravy.

CHAPTER
FOUR

alycon Sage's Post-Event writing projects included *Hat!*, a Post-Modernist Minimalist Neo-Symbolist Pseudo-Realist novel of the same type that had made him internationally famous, except with a punchier title. (See Appendix B for more detail on this work, its inception, composition, and reviews.) Like most other works by Halycon Sage, it is short enough to reproduce here.

Hat!
by Halycon Sage
I thought my hat had shrunk.
But actually, it was the wrong hat.
The End

He liked this one so much that he typed a second copy, then quietly left it at the Dirty Dog, hoping for reactions. (It is possible that one or more persons picked it up and wrote the reviews later discovered by the Squid.) After parasailing through the writer's high of completed work, followed by the inevitable crash, he wrote another.

Stranger

by Halycon Sage

Every time you think life can't get any stranger,

it does. The strangeness is squared, cubed.

What the heck?

The End

In marked contrast to her previous admiration for all his work, Ruby, upon reading this second novel, had given him a withering look. Embarrassed, he deposited it in the wastebasket. Feeling a little shame-faced, he secretly fished it out later and re-read it. Was it really that bad? Was it any worse than his *other* novels, through which he had received worldwide acclaim? Perhaps he had lost his touch, or perhaps Ruby's standards for him had been raised by the completion of his autobiography. He loved her, but sometimes she was a hard taskmistress.

Squid Interlude

Seven, the young techie Squid, was listening to something through his headphones, trying to learn about Earth culture. He had been momentarily distracted by *the new blues hit single that's sweeping the dimensions:* "Ya Gotta Put on Pants!"

The lyrics proceeded as follows.

"Ya gotta put on *pants!* (Uh, uh), ya gotta put on *pants!* (Uh, uh)." Repeated ad nauseum.

While immediately accessible to some, these lyrics were puzzling to many Squids across the galaxies and had generated a great deal of discussion and commentary.

There were also problems with the manufacture of actual *squidpants*, as they were immediately dubbed. Getting the pants to fit was hard enough, what with the difficulties of obtaining tailor's tapes, of measuring underwater or in deep space, and of persuading the squirming young males—it was a predominately male fashion—to stop *writhing* long enough to get accurate measurements. But there was worse to come! As soon as the Squids began moving, their propulsive action and thrashing tentacles kicked the pants *off*, to be lost in the water, sucked into the gravity of a nearby planet, or eaten by a shark. Then it was all to do over again. The Squidish seamstresses were endlessly patient, but it really seemed that their vast talents could have been put to better uses.

The Apocalypse Zombie hit Dry Creek Gulch shortly before sunset on his second day of traveling. He was not hungry or thirsty, having been fortunate to find, within the wagon, a supply of water and a large packet of roast beef sandwiches. They were dried to jerky but perfectly edible thanks to the hot desert sun. He unhitched his mule from the wagon, filled the bucket with water, and tied the reins to a tree, preferring to explore unencumbered.

The first person he saw was little Nuri. The boy was crawling along a dirt path on grubby hands and knees pushing a green metal truck, attempting to replicate the revving and vrooming noises he vaguely remembered from his earlier years. He was also wondering about parallelograms. He took after his father in some ways and his mother in others, besides having hung out with Ratbone and Preisczech, so that his budding awareness encompassed a nice balance of the scientific/mathematical and the literary/historical, along with some plain old childish fun.

After supervising him obsessively for weeks, his parents and other concerned adults had decided he was safe within a block or two of the house and could sometimes be left on his own. The town was a place without traffic and apparently without animal or human predators, and the "eyes on the street" watched over the few precious children as carefully as in some traditional African villages.

At the moment, all these eyes were asleep. If they had seen the moaning Zombie's shambling approach, the adults might have reassessed the situation, but fortunately the meeting was unobserved, and so could unfold in all its natural elegance.

"Greetings," said the Zombie in a sort of rumbling groan.

"Salaam aleykum," responded Nuri, who was still thinking about several things at once and had not quite come back to the material world. *"Kayf al-hal?"* he added, asking politely after the Zombie's health and spirits.

"Aaaarrrrraghghghroarrr," groaned the Zombie, who could make nothing of this.

Nuri collected himself and tried a different approach. "How you bees, Dog?" he inquired, wishing to put the strange-looking visitor at ease.

"Rrrrgggworrhhhaaah!" exclaimed the Zombie, more determined than ever to maintain his role now that communication seemed hopeless. He was reasonably intelligent and would ordinarily have realized that a small boy was not the best place to begin his interactions, but the heat had added an extra layer of confusion to the mental fog produced by the journey, the lack of sleep, and the cessation of several strong drugs at once.

"I grok[2] you, Dude, you're cool," tried Nuri, remembering hippie-toned conversations from before Wolf's retreat into the mountains.

I may be many things, but cool *is not one of them,* thought the Zombie, wiping the sweat from his forehead with a red bandana he'd picked up on the road. *Not in either sense.* Sadly, he realized that he had *never* been cool.

Wanting to emphasize his encouragement and approbation more strongly, Nuri added, "You're smokin', man! Smokin' hot!"

This was one too many for the zombie, and he entered a Halycon Sage-like state of confusion between opposites. The fact that he reacted in this way indicates that he had been more strongly influenced by Sage's works than he had yet realized.

How can I be hot and cool at the same time? Or maybe the kid means I'm literally *smoking.*

"I am?" cried the Zombie, momentarily breaking character and turning circles to see if the back of his ragged clothing was on fire. He had come down to earth with a bump, speculation and embarrassment both forgotten. Nuri had no idea how to respond. He was fresh out of new things to try.

Giving up the whole encounter as a bad job, the Zombie shuffled back the way he had come, making the creaking, groaning noise he had been practicing against his first encounter with human beings. Perhaps he just needed to practice his groaning and shuffling a bit more. His sensitive, though broken, mind shied away from the thought that, at some point, he might actually have to *bite* somebody. That was another problem for another day.

Nuri paused briefly, sadly conscious of his defects as a host. Then he sighed, put one thumb in his mouth, and returned to the contemplation of mathematics, the world in general, and his green metal truck.

CHAPTER

FIVE

age's other new project, apart from *Hat!*, was a novel of unparalleled length and seriousness, at least for him. It was long—longer even than *Boo Radley Goes Hawaiian*—and involved an alternate universe where technology had not been destroyed by the Nanobots, but where alienation was rampant and America had been taken over by a crazy dictator.

As he often did, Sage had begun the new book with a little anecdote that occurred to him, a symptom of the times and the situation he was writing about. From there, the novel would expand. To begin with, he focused on the alienation, rather than the dictator.

In the early twenty-first century, people had become so wedded to their mediated experience—online viewing, internet ordering, and home-delivered meals—that they rarely went out anymore. Even when they did, there were no more friendly little chats with the store clerk about the horrible or wonderful weather or what kind of day anyone was having. A certain energy, a certain flash and sparkle like light, a human-to-human contact, could be transmitted through these commonplace interactions if both so wished. But not anymore.

Now the customer stared at one machine—the bloody little card machine in which a chip reader was or was not activated—while the clerk, two feet away, stared at the computerized cash register to see how the two machines were interacting. Never mind the humans—they were secondary, barely necessary. The following interaction is from real life, and it bore out all of Sage's direst predictions.

Sage: Hey there, pretty hot today, huh?

Clerk: Do you have a rewards card?

Sage (choking back swearing): No, I don't want one. Life is its own reward. (Tries to hand debit card to clerk.)

Clerk (as to an idiot): Put it in the machine.

Sage: Oh.

Alternate events: If Sage slides the card down the side, the clerk says, "Use the chip reader."

If Sage tries to use the chip reader, the clerk says, "Slide it down the side."

Sage makes some feeble joke about never getting to talk to humans anymore. The clerk smiles and nods—

or if a different kind of clerk, looks at him with pity, contempt, or incomprehension.

Sage (in either case): Have a nice day.

I wonder if he's going to write about me, thought Ruby one day with a bit of uncharacteristic discomfort. She was usually unflappable. *I wonder if he's going to write about us.* The thought made her feel shy, another uncharacteristic sensation. Usually, she did not give the back half of a rat what anyone thought of her. Or the back half of *two* rats.

Sage was looking beautiful, asleep on his back, not snoring for once, with his black hair streaming out around him like the tresses of a witch. He had wonderful features, even when his eyes were closed, and his skin was a deep reddish brown, the color an American Indian story cited when describing how some humans were baked too long and burnt by Creator, while others were taken out too soon, underdone and pasty-white. And the third batch came out just right. *Just right,* thought Ruby. *Yes he is.*

CHAPTER

SIX

Halycon Sage's typesetter—in the Alternate Reality, he had a typesetter, though in the real post-Event world he didn't even have a computer—had developed a method of differentiating between Sage's real life adventures, his musings, and the books he was writing. The musings were easy: as long as they were unspoken or mumbled *sotto vocce*, he put them in italics. And he used a different typeface for the novels, so that readers could tell when Sage was making something up and when it was actually happening.

The problem, to which readers of *The Way Beyond* can attest, is that a lot of the time Sage himself didn't know whether he was writing something, living it, or both. It has even been suggested by some of the more interdimensionally minded that Sage was writing his experience *as* he lived it, and some have gone even further by suggesting that he was writing all of *our* experience as well and was, in fact, writing the whole universe as it unfolded. While vehemently disclaiming any God-like qualities this might imply, Sage had to admit that, if true, this would have made him Quite the Dude.

The following is an example of the kind of thing that drove the poor typesetter mad. He had no idea whether the following incident had really happened (Calibri type), or whether Sage was thinking it (italics) or if it was one of his peculiar mini-novels, which had become longer with time, but no less peculiar (type and style to be determined).

And who was this Tarzun, anyway? And who on earth—or off it—was this *Karima Vargas Bushnell?*

Tarzun Refer to Self in Third Person
by Karima Vargas Bushnell
Part 1 of Tarzun Returns:
A Simple Person for Complex Times
(with Apologies to Edgar Rice Burroughs
and Johnny Weissmuller[3])

Does anybody remember the old Tarzan movies starring Johnny Weissmuller? A significant feature was his dialogue, always simple and to the point. "Tarzan hungry!" "Tarzan need Jane!" "Tarzan want Boy clean room now!"

Somehow over a period of years, your humble author has picked up this method of talking to and about herself while accomplishing the simple tasks of the day. "Tarzan mad! Where Tarzan park car?"

As has happened previously with the Halycon Sage characters, this new iteration of Tarzan has gradually assumed a greater solidity and is about to step from the private into the group reality. But since the original Tarzan is already known and loved around the world, we're going to call this guy "Tarzun," which is how both the actor and Jane pronounced it. You'll be hearing from him in the future.

(You will also be hearing from a previously anonymous orange cat, beloved pet of an Iraqi-American family, mentioned briefly in *The Way Beyond*.)

Tarzun is normally a simple being, but one day he made a brief foray into self-reflection, hopefully an isolated incident. Still, he is proud of his intellectual effort and unprecedented spiritual insight and wants to share it with you. This is what he realized: "Tarzun refer to self in third person!"

Kwaheri!

As Sage's books developed to the point of having actual characters, he drew some things from his imagination and some from real life. Tarzun was one of the latter. The Alternate Reality typesetter might not know who Tarzun was, but everybody in Dry Creek Gulch certainly did. You couldn't miss him. His wild yodeling yells began at dawn and echoed through the streets, even though he was living on the edge of town.

Ratbone suspected Tarzun was getting alcohol somewhere—why else would he be acting so oddly? But there was no alcohol left in Dry Creek Gulch. It had all been consumed in one now-legendary post-apocalyptic binge. Some people continued looking for more. Others tried rudimentary homebrew with disappointing results.

Tarzun's stash, if he actually had one, would eventually run out. Maybe then the echoing screeches would end and everybody could get some peace and quiet.

Editor's Interlude

Here, my children, is how Sage's imaginary author was born. One day, Halycon Sage decided to try something different: he would write a book with a female protagonist. Ruby had justly accused his books of being entirely free of women. The books were so short as to be pretty much free of *anybody*, but that was not the point. There was not one woman to be seen, and this was not right. Sage found women interesting, and there was no reason he should not try something in a female voice.

But maybe people would be offended, would say, "What do *you* know about women? You have a lot of nerve, Halycon Sage!"

It was true that nobody in his current time and place seemed to think this way. Only two people were interested in new literature at all, brilliant graduating senior Sophie McGregor and petulant critic Basel Vasselschnauzer, and each currently had other obsessions to occupy them.

Still, it was best to be on the safe side. Sage liked to avoid conflict when possible. He decided that, as well as having a female protagonist, he would write under a female pen name. If George Sand[4] and many others could write in the guise of another gender, then so could he. (How did he know about *her*? Did his forgotten past include some sort of lit major?)

In giving his imaginary author a name, he drew at random from three cultures. This should provide some interesting tensions and contrasts. He would call her Karima Vargas Bushnell—Arabic, Hispanic, and English. It had a certain resonance.

He raised his hands above his typewriter like a concert pianist about to strike the first masterful, perfectly articulated chord and began to write.

Sage felt a vast contentment, the world forgotten. Sentences flowed out. There was no one to bother him, nothing on his mind . . . five minutes later he was rushing out the door, arms filled with his fringed jacket, his typewriter, his guitar, his briefcase, his slide projector, and his medicine bundle. Well, maybe he wasn't really carrying *all* that, but that's what the moment felt like.

To Halycon Sage.

Back at the Dirty Dog—at yet another community meeting—Food had schismed into Hunting and Gathering, Preservation, Raising (of animals), Cooking, and Growing. One of the groups was about to fracture again, there being a bitter conflict between the ovo-lacto-vegetarians, who wanted to treat the local bunnies and western hares as pets, and the more practical and ruthless, who wanted to eat them. Exactly which and how many scruples and finer feelings would survive in the harsh new world was still a question; there was no more ordering out for gluten-free pizza.

Suddenly, Halycon Sage came rushing into the room, dropping things everywhere as usual. He was a big man, and when he was in a hurry, he created chaos. "Has anyone seen No-Name Stupid?"

Nobody had.

At almost the same moment, Ruby walked out of the kitchen, hot-faced and distracted. "Has anyone seen Jenny? She was supposed to help me bake bread today."

Halycon Sage, redirected from his writing to his post-apocalyptic man-job, had recently returned from a hunting trip with former *Times-Enquirer* critic Basel "Deadeye" Vasselschnauzer, whose remarkable UK-trained dart board skills had proven so useful in this new world. The two went on foot, leaving the horse behind, and they had not seen anyone else in days.

Ruby had simply been too absorbed in the thousand tasks of getting the new world on its feet to notice the absence of her friend.

Their eyes met across the room, but because they had already fallen in love and were as good as married, the glance was not one of *those* across-a-crowded-room encounters. Rather, it was a glance of consternation, a realization that a disquieting amount of time had passed since anyone had seen Jenny, or Preisczech, or No-Name Stupid.

45

CHAPTER
SEVEN

Where they were, and
more about the Blue Thread

If you can't identify it, it's probably a squid.
This has been a public service message.

"I'm surprised nobody else notice." Preisczech, in his heavy accent, was talking to pass the time. The couple and No-Name Stupid had been walking the desert foothills for several days, well-provisioned with sturdy backpacks and saddlebags. "Is very strange, but nobody notice."

"Well, they're very busy," said Jenny judiciously. "They haven't got time to think. Except your friend Sage, and he's probably writing another book."

"Is surely true for sure," said Preisczech. His English had improved vastly, but it was still odd and still dropped off to not very much when he was tired. Jenny didn't mind. She always understood him.

"So odd," continued Preisczech. "We have water here, solar power, we grow things in glass tunnels. Very nice set-up, very nice. Why nobody come to take?"

"Maybe they're all dead," said Jenny gently. She had given this matter a lot of thought. There had been no bodies, yet the population was vastly reduced. If it had indeed been the Rapture expected by some—a winnowing process of removing the good people and discarding the bad—it had left a surprisingly pleasant and cooperative society behind. Though she had access to a bigger picture that would have astounded those who knew her, Jenny was not exactly clear on the smaller details of how all this had come about.

"Three weeks, four weeks, how many come? Two. *Two!* That Tarzun nutball and that Apocalypse Zombie— even crazier. How come? Maybe nobody else can get through? Maybe some kind of invisible barrier?"

"What, do you think those two have special powers?" After the events of the last few weeks, nothing would surprise her.

"Yeah, right. Power to swing through trees yelling. And power to make people throw up their lunch." Preisczech took a swig of water and felt his concentration return.

"If we don't find something soon, we go home."

They had been traveling for days, but all they had found was desert and mountains. Sage, pine, and tough manzanita bushes with shiny green leaves and mahogany-looking stems you couldn't break. Some tumbleweeds, which always made Preisczech wax nostalgic. Some beautiful birds and animals. But no explanation for the fact that, though Dry Creek Gulch was only about two hours from a large city, no one had come from outside to disturb their post-apocalypse idyll.

And just like that, the improbable thing occurred.

No-Name Stupid, who was walking slightly ahead, bounced off an invisible wall and recoiled backward with an offended neigh. He did not like being put out of his dignity.

They had found the Perimeter.

While Preisczech, Jenny, and No-Name Stupid were discovering the perimeter wall and the Ruby/Sage contingent was searching for them, the ship was drawing nearer to the Earth, and the passionate discussion among the Squidren had reached the matter of finding names for themselves. It appeared that each Earther had an individual personal name, sometimes more than one; to omit this in the construction of their culturally appropriate characters would be a grave error. It had been impressed on them again and again by the Elder that they must make themselves as like the Earthers as possible, so that their message would be heard.

So now they were trying to decide on a personal name for each, taking into account the historical, geographical, and cultural significance of the various Earthean groups and which were most important. The discussion was fraught with intensity. Unfortunately for future intercultural relations, the Squid were, as usual, more concerned with the *sound* of their discussion than with its factual conclusions.

Look at England.
But look at China.
But look at England.
But look at China.
Africa, the Middle East . . . the Americas.
Japan, though small,
is forceful, fierce and clever.
We are leaving many out.
But look at China.

They stopped. The tone and rhythm of their conversation pleased them. The effort was complete. Now they moved to the most important phase of any discussion: the silent, though shared, contemplation of its music. The matter had been decided. Each Squid would choose zi's own name.

CHAPTER

EIGHT

"Stay back, Jenny. This could be dangerous."

Jenny forbore to inform her husband that she had survived dangers which would curl his hair—well, it was curly already, but never mind that. She had not yet told him everything. He would have been horrified and would probably have worried and sulked for weeks. She stood discretely away, addressing the immediate priority of comforting the stunned horse. No-Name Stupid had been practically knocked off his legs. While still somewhat dazed, he appeared to be injured in his dignity rather than his physical body.

I knew this was a bad idea, thought No-Name Stupid. He'd given no credence to wild rumors of people's reluctance or inability to leave town in certain directions or to the even wilder claim by one human nut-job of running smack into an invisible wall. When these topics arose during meetings, Stupid, listening at an open window, grew bored and wandered away.

Preisczech approached the peculiar barrier. Nothing could be seen except a faint shimmering in the air. But it was rock solid. His cautious investigations showed that it produced no shock. Stupid had been stunned, not by any force issuing from the wall, but by his own clumsiness and inattention in walking right into it.

Though, to be fair, besides the faint shimmer, there was nothing to be seen but the country beyond the wall, which was very similar to the country they had come from. Too similar.

Preisczech looked forward and behind, forward and behind, testing his hypothesis like the good scientist he was. Yup. (He was proud of this little Americanism, this little Westernism). Yup. The thing was a *mirror*. Though it didn't reflect *themselves* at all, which made it kind of a funny one. Moving silently, they began following the wall[5].

A few hours later, Sage and Ruby came around a little hill beside the winding trail, and suddenly there they were: Stupid, Jenny, and Preisczech. The two parties greeted each other with relief. Preisczech was the most excited, eager to show off his find.

"Look, Sage! Is Perimeter Wall!"

"Come again?" inquired Sage. He was not actually *slow*, as he occasionally appeared. Rather, he usually had to come back from a long way away. His habitual and simultaneous tracking of fact, fantasy, everyone's emotions, and several alternating realities and dimensions, which might or might not turn out to be real, took up a lot of his attention and sometimes made him appear clueless.

"Is Perimeter Wall! Goes around, you see? We think, *all* around. We have walked it for miles."

"We think this is why we've only had two visitors since the Event," broke in Jenny. "Nobody else can get in!"

Sage considered this. It made sense. He too had been troubled by the absence of arriving strangers, but he'd had other fish to fry and had pushed the thoughts away.

"So, we're prisoners?" he inquired calmly.

Preisczech had thought about this aspect too (and incidentally, his English had suddenly returned). "I don't think so. Remember Wolf and those guys that went into the hills camping? Still out there, I think. Some other people have left, too. And then all those people *came down* from the hills, all those mountain men and computer geeks." He paused, calculating. All those arrivals had been in the first few days. Nobody had shown up since, except the two crazies.

"We can still get out, I think. It's just that nobody wants to. Why *would* you?"

Sage agreed. The situation at Dry Creek Gulch was practically perfect. It couldn't be better if he'd written it himself.

They stood still, enjoying the smells of the desert air, the gentle breeze on the cheek, the brilliant sun. If you were born here, or had moved here and fallen in love with it, you never got tired of these things. If you were born here, the heat and light were no problem. You merely soaked them in like a contented lizard or, in times of real necessity, wore a hat or sunglasses. Sage almost always wore a hat, but Preisczech never did. He had had mild sunstroke a couple of times and rather enjoyed it. It gave him new ideas, a new point of view. Of course, Preisczech was crazy. You couldn't take his advice on these practical matters.

A new shimmer began to appear, like the faint, ghostly shimmer of the Perimeter Wall, but stronger, more noticeable. It slowly solidified into a bright silver shape that reminded No-Name Stupid of something. It looked like two slightly elongated oval dishes with their edges meeting in the middle, on the horizontal plane. Stupid considered this. *The horizontal plane*, he thought. *What an elegant concept*!

Jenny, Preisczech, and Stupid watched in fascination, waiting to see what would happen next. Their peculiar combination of different types of intelligence, cluelessness, and confidence prevented any hysteria, any panicky retreat.

A vertical oval area on the side of the thing facing them began to look different from its surrounding material. It was growing thinner. It became translucent, then it was gone, leaving a large gap. Large enough for something—someone?—to step through.

What emerged was a good bit taller than Sage, maybe seven feet. It was of a pleasing purpley blue color, and, like everything else connected with this situation from the wall to the spaceship to the desert itself, it gave off a shimmer, like the sunlight of a Nevada dawn catching an awakening sprinkler system. Watery beads of light seemed to come from the thing, a fine spray of brilliance. With it came an atmosphere of hope and joy. Having no idea how the rest of the town would react to the newcomer, the little party beside the wall were already big fans.

Oh, and it had eight arms and two tentacles. It was a squid.

CHAPTER
NINE

First Contact

"I'm John Kennedy," said the Squid, stepping forward. Well, slithering. A few others had arrived quietly behind him. Halycon Sage stood silent. Though his amnesia had blocked the time and place, he had absorbed extensive training in good manners as seen in the Indian way. If you did not understand something, you kept silent. You waited for the meaning to appear, for comprehension to dawn. It was also respectful to leave pauses after someone spoke. It was wrong to leap in immediately, showing yourself to be a fool: brash, rude, and thoughtless.

The silence grew.

A minute-and-a-half can seem like forever at the first meeting of alien races. The Squid stood frozen, as if in a game of statues. Jenny and Preisczech, a little back from the group, watched with interest, his arm around her shoulders.

Finally, the tension became unbearable. Something had to be done, and Sage made the decision to meet like with like.

He stepped forward. "I'm Pope Francis."

John Kennedy was certainly an odd name for a Squid from beyond the galaxy, but the Squid had been so intent on their own peculiar form of linguistics that their practical research had been, perhaps, inadequate.

Seeing that a successful two-sentence exchange had at last been achieved, the rest of the Squidren stepped forward and introduced themselves in like manner.

"I'm John Chang."

"I'm Mohammed Schmidt."

"I'm Muhammad Wang Smith."

"I'm Obiwan Mohammed."

At that moment, when it seemed that nothing weirder could happen, Preisczech stepped forward. He was full of joy. He remembered his long, agonizing experience in picking out a name that would help him blend into an unfamiliar land, earning him respect and credibility. He remembered his many missteps and rejections, and the humiliating laughter. Maybe his long, painful search for a name was not without meaning, not the absurd caprice of a cruel, uncaring universe without any organizing moral principal. He could guide these strangers, spare them the pain he had gone through, welcome them graciously when they had come so far.

He could be a bridge, a mentor, an example in this matter of names.

Preisczech held out his hand and clasped a faintly pulsing tentacle. "I'm Alexander Flintstone Lazlo Buddy Macadamian Preisczech,[2]" he said, with the deep assurance of one who knows his way.

Amid all the drama of the last half hour, almost no one had noticed a strange thing: not strange in the way of invisible shimmering barriers and landings of alien races, but strange in the more ordinary way of someone acting entirely out of character.

Jenny sidled unobtrusively up to Ruby. From the first faintly glowing appearance of the spaceship, and maybe from earlier than that, Ruby had not said a single word. Sure, Ruby was quiet, a woman of action, not of words. But still.

"Are you alright?" asked Jenny, her voice softly concerned.

There was no better friend than Jenny, Ruby had discovered, concealing an iron-hard resilience and strength beneath a gentle and feminine exterior. Ruby, though equally beautiful, was thin, bronzed, and tough.

---

2   *Why Macadamian, you ask? Having steeped yourself in the first Chronicle, you doubtless remember that the original name in question had been "Buddy Mac," not "Buddy Macadamian". But remember also, that Preisczech, though slightly odd, was a genius. And his conversations with Halycon Sage had increased his sensitivity to the rhythm and texture of words a thousandfold. At this moment, he knew instinctively that "Buddy Mac" would offend the Squid deeply. It did not scan.

One would have expected them to hate each other on sight, but such was not the case.

"Yeah, I'm fine," she said. "But assuming they're not cannibals—human-eaters, I mean, that wouldn't make them cannibals, would it? But putting that possibility aside," she lapsed into what used to be called a brown study. A quick one.

"Yes?" said Jenny, curious as to what could be important enough to distract her friend from the drama of the immediate situation.

Ruby looked her straight in the eye. "What the hell are we going to offer them for dinner?"

The frantic pre-dinner discussion around what, exactly, to feed the squid, and how to ask without offending them, went something like this, different voices chiming in.

"What about fish? If they're squid, they live in the ocean, right? So they must eat fish." Abdurrahim had spent time on the Mediterranean and was fond of fish.

"Yeah, but they breathe air and walk around on land. Not exactly typical sea creatures!" That was Ratbone, observant and practical as always.

"Well, anyway. Maybe they eat plankton. And seaweed and stuff."

"Eww."

"Thank you, Nuri, now is not the time. Why don't we just ask them?"

"But what if we say something horribly offensive? What if the fish are their friends, or the plankton, for that matter? They could decide we're no good and wipe us off the planet, destroy the Earth." One of the worry warts, found in every crowd.

"It's pretty well destroyed already, isn't it?" Ruby, another practical one.

"Well, we don't know, that's the whole point. The only outside visitors have been Tarzun and the Apocalypse Zombie, and neither of them has enough brains to explain how they got here, let alone report on conditions outside."

"Zombie, brains, hahahaha." Someone had evidently been telling Nuri old movies as bedtime stories.

"Nuri, you are becoming far too American! A little politeness, please!"

"Geez Layla, that's pretty harsh."

"No offense intended. My heartiest apologies!"

"Here's the real point: Do we think the Squid are the ones who made the barrier wall? Are they the ones keeping us in?"

"Not us *in*, everyone else *out!* Haven't you been paying attention? We could all walk out whistling Dixie, and there's nothing to stop us."

"Are you kidding? You should have seen Stupid hit that wall. He bounced back!"

"*You* didn't see it!" An indignant Preisczech.

"But you described it so beautifully!"

"Sage, you've gotta stop missing the meetings. Yeah, I know, you're writing the Great Apocalypse Novel.

But you gotta pay attention. There's free access out at the highway, and at the dirt road at the other end of town. We can get out, but nobody can get in." While the two couples and the horse had been conducting their searches, those left behind had also been making discoveries, or at least evolving new theories.

Several voices broke in at once. "How do you know that?" "Has anybody tried?" "And what makes you think those exits aren't just part of the area *within* the Perimeter Wall? It's a pretty big area, miles, maybe *hundreds* of miles!" "Yeah, what makes you think it ends outside the city limits in just those two directions?" "Well, if you'd *been* at the *meeting*..."

Ruby enacted one of those compelling silences certain strong personalities can impose with merely a look, a change of expression, a faint body motion.

"So, what are we going to feed these squid?"

CHAPTER

TEN

The dinner was awkward, and why wouldn't it be? To start with, the Squid didn't sit. For another thing, their rules of precedence regarding who should be placed next to whom, what part of the table was the power position, and who should occupy it were all incomprehensible.

Anthony, formerly known as Buzzard of the Dirty Dog Gang, had the nicest house in town, so the dinner meeting was held there[3]. Several of the more important Squid were present at the dinner, as well as minor Squid in the capacity of servants, waiters, or junior colleagues—none of the Earthers was quite sure which.

Notably present were John Kennedy, Muhammad Wang Smith, John Chang, and Lol-Bey. Lol-Bey's name unfortunately occasioned some unintended mirth on

---

3 Son of the wealthiest woman in town, Buzzard had finally revealed his identity in response to the desperate plight of the Iraqi family, who now lived with him part time. There were so many rooms it made little difference. Layla and her husband had assumed the majority of the household chores.

the part of Ratbone, who nearly sprayed soup upon hearing it.

"Lol Bey? Does that mean you're a Moorish Scientist, and we're supposed to laugh at you? Cause you don't look like no Turk from the Ottoman Empire! And you're certainly not my baby!"

Ratbone was well read and self-educated in an eccentric way, an autodidact with far ranging interests, and all his interpretations of Bey were correct. It added to his confusion that the Squidren had misread LOL as a common Earth name. Fortunately, neither the Squids nor anyone else at the table understood what he was talking about enough to be insulted.

We draw a veil over exactly what was served. If you're really that curious, you might consult the *Encyclopedia Galactica*[6] if you can find an updated version. We have more pressing information to impart.

Many things happened at the dinner, but only two had far reaching effects. Arguably only one, but Sophie et al., the researchers studying the Squid, maintain that the little speech made by Lol-Bey, a junior Squid, was the first break into understanding Squidian culture. Here is that story, seen from his point of view.

What Lol-Bey Did, and What He Thought About It

Though nothing about the Earthers had really disturbed him, Lol-Bey was uneasy about the Que-kombers that were served with dinner. While they were clearly not forbidden, he thought it better to make the *Prayer of Kind Intention* for them.

"Oh, Little Brothers," he intoned. "You have made great strides toward individuation. You have attained faces, a thing to which many single and multi-celled organisms have barely aspired! Know that your lives were not in vain! May you attain Personality! May you be raised Beyond Yourselves! May it be so!"

He looked up to find the Earthers at the table observing him oddly or edging away nervously. He shrugged. "Well, *look* at them." He shrugged again. And a shrug on a Squid is something to see.

The second thing that happened was The Gift of the Cuttlefish.

This was a special moment, and Muhammad Wang Smith, John Chang, Lol-Bey, and the rest watched intently, as did a strange little Squid who was lurking in the corner. Unlike everyone else from the ship, this one was flat, monochromatic black, not glistening, not luminescent. But somehow every eye slid away from zi. No one was even interested.

John Kennedy had chosen his name both to honor a much admired Earthean president and to signal his own primacy. He had many important functions, both practical and ceremonial, and this was one: upon leaving the hosted meal given by the Earthers—at least he presumed it had been a meal—it was his duty as commander to Give the Gift.

The Gift must exemplify the Five Characteristics, which echoed the colors of the Braided Thread, one of the most sacred concepts in *The Book of Lighted Squid*. This gift was perfect. It expressed Life (Green Thread, and it was undoubtedly alive), Water (Blue Thread, also signifying certain types of emotion, spirituality, and music), and Light (Yellow Thread, and it had the luminosity characteristic of most things and beings originating on the Squid Planet). It also included the Red Thread (energy, impetus, certain *different* types of emotion, spirituality, and music). Although its exposition of the Black Thread was more subtle, there being no actual black color anywhere upon its surface, it would be the Essence of Mystery to these Earthers, and as everyone knows, mystery, in the deepest and most holy sense, is the Essence of the Black Thread.

Further, it could take its Honored Friend on a journey such as few in any dimension or galaxy could imagine, if only the Bond was established and the Friend was found worthy.

The moment had arrived. The eating was complete, and the guests were poised to depart. John Kennedy stood and addressed the youngest member of the Earthean contingent, the proper recipient of the Guesting Gift according to the ancient protocols. "Honored Sir, I have for thee a gift, brought from far away. The Gift of the Cuttlefish."

There was silence as everyone present inhaled the fragrance of this climactic moment, the Sealing Ceremony of the newborn friendship between two alien races, as august and unlikely as the meeting of stars, and as cataclysmic, for good or ill.

Everyone was silent with holy awe, even the Earthers . . . or were they?

Their facial expressions were remarkably blank, perhaps through an effort to suppress their almost insurmountable emotion at being present here, at the peak experience of many lifetimes.

Nuri, for of course he was the youngest, reached out a trembling hand. If any Earther present understood what was going on, it was Nuri. This gift was a friend, a strange creature worthy of all awe and respect and love, brought to him from across the stars and dimensions. And he would be worthy. He would be worthy.

"Oh, that looks *good!* When do we *eat it?*" exclaimed someone, stepping forward eagerly, trying hard to show enthusiasm while dubiously examining the writhing creature in the little, hand-held tank.

We will not reveal who made this blunder. It wasn't Halycon Sage, anyway, and it wasn't Basel Vasselschnauzer, either. *And it certainly wasn't me,* thought No-Name Stupid when he heard the story later.

Nuri did not wait to hear the reaction of the Squids or the consternation of the Earthers once they realized their mistake, to witness the confusion, the shock, the embarrassment, the humiliation. Bursting into tears, he ran into his room and slammed the door. He was never this rude, never a door slammer, but he pretty much couldn't bear it. He lay face down on his bed, a small puddle of human misery.

"Habibi! Habibi!" cried Layla, flying into his room and scooping him up in a motherly hug. "It will be alright! It will be alright! I know it!"

"How can you know, *Umi*, how can you know?" sobbed the boy.

"*Subhanallah*[7]," said Layla quietly. "I know. I know." And the funny thing about it? She did.

He grew calmer, his sobs lessening, and as sleep came at last, he heard his mother slip from the room.

A little while later he awoke with a pleased, drowsy sensation that someone else had been there. He felt calm and sure. The impression was still with him of a blue and faintly glowing tentacle reaching over his head. He looked at the place where the tentacle had touched the bed, somewhere past his right shoulder.

The tentacle had left something. It was a book, and it was open. Like everything else to do with the Squid, it had a faint effervescent glow. Only one thing was printed there, a simple verse like a nursery rhyme. Nuri, unbeknownst to anyone, peered into *The Book of Lighted Squid*.

He read:
Cuttlefish, cuddle fish
Snuggly, buggly cuddle fish
Shall you eat it in a dish?
Don't you touch my cuttlefish!

The word *touch* seemed somehow to be written in fiery letters. It contained a warning and perhaps also a *warding*, in the old, magical sense. It would be a foolish person indeed who would attempt to injure Nuri's Friend.

CHAPTER
ELEVEN

The Squid had been less apparent since the dinner-party debacle. While limited contact continued, they no longer walked openly in public. Because the dinner had occurred the same day as First Contact, not everyone had seen them, and the spectrum of public opinion ranged from intrigued acceptance to total disbelief. Some still considered the Squidren no more than another wild rumor from the post-Apocalypse silly season.

The following appeared early one morning on the large community notice board at the ~~Dirty Dog Bar~~ Canis Fidelis Grill and Juice Bar: two stapled pages carefully torn from a notebook, covered with typing, and attached with a thumb tack at the corner.

A Guide to the Squidren Vol. 1: for the Edification, Preparation, and Information of the Remaining World Civilization

Sophie MacGregor et al.
Rough Draft

My colleagues and I have gathered all available information regarding the Squidren here under one cover, that is, between two covers. Unless the tack won't hold up the covers, in which case: between no covers. While it is not much, it is far better than the complete mystery (except for their physical appearance) that previously engulfed them in human eyes. Please study it carefully. It may save your life!

The facts below are currently arrayed in the order in which they were discovered, or by topic. Some discussion is ongoing as to which method will best serve the final presentation.

<u>To Whom It May Concern</u>: Everyone please read this! It is of vital importance that we gather and share all possible knowledge of the Squidren (Squids, plural, but only properly used for groups of 12 or more). My team has been working on this, and these are the first fruits of our results.

You may say these observations (which have been carefully tested) are small and unimportant, but any new fact may lead to a breakthrough in understanding this extremely alien culture. If you have any direct knowledge of Squiddish customs or behavior not included here, please contact us immediately! A second edition of this publication will be reaching you soon. So, while this is actually a scholarly paper—bit of a pun here—we're issuing it in its initial form as a *paper* in the sense of a *newspaper*. Thank you for your attention.

At this point there was a blank space where someone had written,

Nobody's gonna read all this!
What you should have said is:
IMPORTANT INFO RE: SQUID!!!

The paper continued:

<u>Things We Know about the Squidren</u>

1. The plural of Squid is Squidren, but this is generally not used for groups of fewer than twelve. The words Squid or Squids are sometimes used as plurals in casual conversation.
2. While Squid groupings of twelve or over are formally referred to as Squidren, members of a group of between two and eleven, inclusive, are

often called Squidiler. (Pronounced squid-IH-LEHR. Yes, like a Turkish plural.) Note: these rules for plurals are not entirely reliable! (Might these variations be due to Squidish regional or hierarchical differences?)

3. The Squidren apparently have three genders (possibly more). Two of these correspond to male and female. The third is not yet fully understood by our scientists (i.e., the present authors).

4. The Squidren consider the acts of speaking and writing very important but do not judge the success or failure of these communication acts by exactly the same criteria that humans would use.

5. While he/him and she/her may be safely used for the more familiar Squid genders, members of the Squidren's third gender are referred to as zi (pronounced zee), which functions as both a subject and an object. Also used if gender is unknown.

6. Physical description: Based on the observations of a limited number of individuals, Squid range from seven to ten feet in height and come in differingly accented shades of medium to dark fluorescent blue, some shading to green and others to purple. They stand upright and appear to flow or swim over the ground without putting any weight on it. (Color appears to relate to

gender, but can be temporarily affected by other factors, such as intense emotion.)

7. The Squid seem a bit touchy about being referred to as he, she, or zi. It is important to get this right.

8. Zi is also used for God (capitalized), and without the capital for any being that is sentient, but whose gender is undetermined or for unidentified members of mixed-gender groups. (The Squid equivalent of a capital letter is too complex to address here.)

   Note: There is currently disagreement among myself and my colleagues as to whether the following two rules (9 and 10) should be eventually listed under Squid Linguistics or Squid Religion. Or both, which is my contention. As it only makes sense. And covers all the facts. As the other purported solutions do not.

9. When the squid are typing (?) on their computers and they have to backspace or otherwise erase a letter, a small ritual prayer is said, assuring the letter that its existence was real, valid, and important, though momentary, and has not been in vain.

10. Within Squidish culture, if you have the choice of erasing a letter, word, or phrase and typing it again or of cutting it and pasting it elsewhere, always choose the latter, preserving it in its integrity of being, respecting it, and prolonging its life.

11. In bed at night, if you shove your foot far enough under a cat, it will come out the other side and you will then have a place to put your foot. Your instinct will be to pull your foot back. The cat will be warm and heavy and you'll be reluctant to wake him. Do not give in to these fears! Persevere!

Dear Colleague!!! Please check your work more carefully. This last rule is obviously your note <u>on some other topic</u> that got in here by mistake. Sloppiness like this could lead to serious consequences. —Sophie

To be continued.

———

Only one response appeared on the board other than the criticism of the introductory paragraph, but it was a doozy.

Sophie! Do you realize what this means??
Forget all that junk about words.
THE SQUID HAVE COMPUTERS!

The correspondent was evidently excited and forgot to leave their name. Sophie was a bit embarrassed that, being caught up in the fascinating rules of Squidish religion and etymology, she had completely missed this important point.

PART TWO

THE ZIKR

WHEREIN the Black Thread is unveiled and illumined.
Black is the Essence of Mystery.

CHAPTER
TWELVE

*Remember Wolf and those guys
that went into the hills camping?
Still out there, I think.* —Alexander Preisczech

While in some parts of the country, including most of the West and the northern prairie and forest state of Minnesota, "guys" generically includes both women and men, these guys were indeed *guys*, and guy-like, they had given themselves a macho-sounding name. There had been some discussion about whether to be the Force (the Star Wars faction), the Pack (werewolf buffs) or the Troop (everybody else). The Troop eventually prevailed.

Among others, the Troop included Snake Eyes, Beaner, and Skull, previously of the Dirty Dog Gang; Rap, Sparky, and Big D, previously of the Fifth Street Mofos; and some former internet geeks in their teens and twenties. Most of this latter group were now aspiring mountain men. The accidental viewing of a movie called *Jeremiah Johnson* shortly before the Event had stuck in their minds, providing a competing interest, which under post-Event conditions (no more tech!) easily overcame the ubiquitous Sci-Fi/gaming obsession.

All in all, the Troop got along pretty well, though there were some casual scuffles and minor fistfights. Their initial focus was on survival—shelter, water, fire, food—and unlike Preisczech, they got the order right. Mere survival in the foothills beneath the majestic snow-capped mountains precluded most of the rivalries and general silliness that would otherwise have infected so varied an assemblage.

Much to his own surprise, the once unassuming and rather tentative Wolf had emerged as a sort of elder statesman and one of the leaders. He hadn't done much obvious leading in the Dirty Dog Gang, but he had always been the sort who steps up when no one else is willing or able.

Rap (so-called because he *could*), formerly number two man to Ratbone, was strongly built, of medium height, quick and clever. He was the other leader. The relationship between Rap and Wolf was symbiotic and easy, based on a mutual tendency to put practical matters and the good of the group ahead of personal interests.

So far things were working out well. Everyone was pitching in. Sparky had been convinced that, while a tendency to set random fires might be alright in some situations, it could not be tolerated in the dry western hills. He tended the campfire, which he viewed with superstitious awe since it was keeping them all alive. In this task, he was closely supervised by Big D, who was vigilant and smarter than he looked.

How to Write a Novel was a little jewel Halycon Sage had originally found at Sundance Books in Reno and was now studying assiduously. As previously mentioned, when everyone had wanted him to be a writer, he had hated it, but as soon as no one cared, he was all dedication.

The introduction to *How to Write a Novel* told him that each character should have no more than three attributes. Two of them should go together, while the third should be contradictory, building interest. You should also mention each character's height and hair color so that readers could tell them apart. It was important to give the characters *different* heights and hair colors. If everyone was medium height with brown hair, it would be necessary to make them speak and think differently, and how much of a sweat was *that?*

There were even TEN RULES to help the aspiring author, and despite his former celebrity, Sage was feeling a bit like a novice since only now was he actually learning his craft. His previous worldwide success had been a fluke.

The rules began:

 Rule 1. Write reams of nonsense, it's fine! You can always hack it down later.

 Rule 2. Never put too many redheads in one book!

 Rule 3. (a) Write your first book, polish it lovingly, then throw it in the trash.

 (b) Write your second book.

The author was one Kilgore Trout[8], and Sage was almost certain he had heard the name somewhere, that Trout was known to everyone and had published many novels of great consequence. The fact that all his friends said, "Kilgore who?" did not deter him.

It was pretty widely assumed that Jenny had a secret, and since she was well-liked, there was a general tendency among the townsfolk not to mention it or even think about it too much. From some things she had said, but much more from what she had *not* said, they had come to certain conclusions. Perhaps they had gotten the idea from the suggestive song that had led Preisczech to her in the first place[9]. Jenny had shown up at the Dirty Dog shortly before the Event, wearing too much makeup and looking fragile. She had arrived just in time to fall in love with Preisczech, fulfilling all his dreams. Their subsequent marriage had been idyllic.

Though brilliant in some areas, the scientist who had invented the Nanobots and brought down world technology was singularly obtuse in others. Nobody wanted to mention to him that sweet, innocent Jenny might have been a member of the oldest profession fleeing a bad situation, or at least a young lady of pretty wide experience. He would not have understood.

Jenny herself was reticent about her past, only admitting in private that, before the end of the world, she had played a far different role than she did now, had been through harrowing experiences with some rough characters, and had borne a different name.

Jenny *did* have a secret, but it was miles away from what everyone suspected.

CHAPTER
THIRTEEN

Introducing the Orangey-Yellow Thread

At the outset, some threads might
seem trivial, unconnected.
Childish, even.
This is not the case.
Everything is part of the Great Braid.
Only be patient. You shall see.
— From The Book of Lighted Squid

Okay, so it's supposed to be the Yellow Thread, so sue me. Or start an inquisition, convict me of insulting *The Book of Lighted Squid*. But we have to adapt to new planets and new cultures, and the greatest representative of the Yellow Thread on Planet Earth, in Halycon Sage's universe, is not yellow, but orange—well, orange-and-white *striped*. Just as it says in the quote above, *'you shall see.'*

-Anonymous Squid

✺

Tired from the sustained effort of writing his Really Serious Novel about the Alternate universe and the dictator and the alienation and all, Halycon Sage decided to write something silly. He had noticed that, while profundity apparently dripped from his fingertips when he tossed off one of his two-sentence novels— at least according to the more gushing reviewers—any actual attempt to write something strong and meaningful produced a great wodge of undigested words like soggy paper towels. Far from taking flight and inspiring the masses, this wodge lay on the ground like a beached whale, inciting universal indifference.

He thought a moment.

He would write about cats!

With pictures!

Cats were very popular on the internet, which was probably still active in the Alternate Universe. And actually, the only cat he knew, Nuri's orange stripy number, was already popular and up to interesting things. That cat had a few tricks up his sleeve. Sage decided to write about *him*.

In other literary news, Halycon Sage's imaginary author, 'Karima Vargas Bushnell', was beginning to annoy him. For one thing, she had continued to evolve and now had too many characteristics, violating the three-attribute rule from *How to Write a Novel*. In reacting against the terse minimalism that had made him famous, Sage had taken to gilding the lily. His author was Muslim—since meeting Abdurraheem, Sage had grown interested in the religion—but also played Irish music. She was a sweet old lady with cats and simultaneously an international woman of mystery, beautiful beyond description and with a terrible temper. She lived in frumpy Minnesota but came from flashy Reno, admiring big hair and long, red fingernails. She had been a college professor, a county court reporter, a hippie, and, long ago in her pre-Muslim days, had sold beer and hotdogs at the Santa Cruz auto races.

This character was ridiculous, and nobody would believe her.

Sage was nothing if not self-contradictory, and his character shared this characteristic. Could he write "character" and "characteristic" in the same phrase? And if she was an author, how could she be a *character*?

Puzzled, Halycon Sage gave up and went to make himself a baloney sandwich. Ever addicted to terrible food, he had a secret stash of baloney and Wonder Bread concealed in a far corner of the deep cave where supplies needing refrigeration were kept. Nobody knew.

Suddenly, Sage, always an aficionado of worlds within worlds and mirrors reflecting mirrors, had the most scathingly brilliant idea: 'Karima Vargas Bushnell' could be writing a book about *Halycon Sage*!

Knowing his own tendency to confuse fact and fiction, Sage always put this character's name in single quotes to remind himself that she wasn't real. He had tried to make her his opposite—white, female, and short—but their personalities were disturbingly similar. With some dismay, he realized that he had created an alter ego.

Interlude: Tarzun and the Apocalypse Zombie

As different as they were, Tarzun and the Apocalypse Zombie had more in common than being the only new arrivals and two of the strangest denizens of the new world. The main similarity was that both had decided they could be whoever they wanted.

Gone was the need for Social Security numbers, passports, or identifying information of any kind. Gone also was the elaborate web of tracking and surveillance that connected computers, video cams, and spy apparatus around the world. None of that stuff worked any more. If one of them had said he was Leonardo DaVinci and the other had claimed to be Mary Magdalene, nobody could have proven them wrong.

The other thing they had in common was that both had reached the outskirts of Dry Creek Gulch but had stopped short of fully integrating into the population, instead camping out in houses on the eastern and western ends of town, respectively. They were motivated both by embarrassment at their oddness and by a desire to perfect their skills before fully unveiling their new characters. While posses from the forage committee had scoured the nearer houses for edible food and clean water, they had succeeded in finding enough that the ends of town had mostly been ignored. Scouts would come eventually, but for now, these remoter areas were undisturbed.

The Zombie's white clapboard house, though dilapidated, had a shady porch, and the residents had evidently been backpackers, or maybe survivalists. There was a large supply of freeze-dried food in the basement and many large containers of water. There was also a garden. If it rained a bit and the Zombie lasted that long, there would eventually be fresh vegetables.

Tarzun had also found everything he needed in or around the little adobe-style house he had staked out. Several large trees with sturdy branches were perfect for him to practice his swinging and climbing. He wrongly assumed that no one was within earshot to be bothered by his raucous yells. Water could be hauled from a nearby pond. What Tarzun ate was a mystery—perhaps he was eating bugs to supplement the onions, potatoes, and withered apples he found in the basement, getting into his ape-man role, as it were.

From this point on, their characters diverged. The Zombie, an intelligent but somewhat limited young man who had majored in art and worked himself into a nervous breakdown, was motivated by pure practicality. He was limited in the sense that his personal interests were narrow and always had been. Also, his memory had been badly affected by psychiatric drugs and other medical tinkering. Putting together the few facts he knew or could observe about himself and the world, he had come up with this obvious role. His ideas had developed along the following lines.

Upon awakening, he had seen that there was a hole in the wall of his institutional bedroom, leading right out into the hospital garden. His presence in a private room indicated some degree of wealth. There was no sign of other patients or staff, so apparently he could go where and when he liked. The constant hum of electricity was gone, replaced by the sounds of birds and the silent sunshine. Clearly the Apocalypse had come—not in some religious sense, but in the sense of The End of the World as We Knew It.

Before his hospital admission and after his precipitous retreat from college, his broken mind had been steeped in computer games, online role-playing, and science fiction. *Cogito ergo sum. Or cogito esse est*, or something like that. *Quod erat demonstradum*. This was the Apocalypse.

He had arisen from his bed and looked in the full-length mirror behind the door, cracked, but still useable. Yeah, he looked weird enough. The shuffling gate, the flapping nightgown, the vacant eyes. His bandaged, scarred, lopsided face, covered with hideous, uneven white patches. Zombies were a necessary part of any good Apocalypse. He was the Apocalypse Zombie.

Tarzun's motivations were almost diametrically opposed. He was a dreamer and a fantasist. Growing up in the snow and ice of Minnesota, he dreamed of tropical jungles. The Zombie, who had traveled, could have given him a good reason for staying out of the tropics, but never mind that for now. Tarzun's mother, from Washington, D.C., had a saying, "The palm longs for the pine and the pine for the palm." In other words, you romanticized and wanted to be wherever it was you weren't. This was certainly true in his case. Older than the Apocalypse Zombie by decades, he had grown up on *Tarzan, Zorro, The Prisoner of Zenda*, and *The Lone Ranger*[10]. Not the modern versions, but the real stuff, from the 1960s or before. If his grasp on reality ever improved, he'd be on a collision course with Halycon Sage on the subject of Tonto, but any such controversy was far in the future, one of the more remote possibilities along some disused timeline.

Of all the old heroes, books, and shows, his favorite was Tarzan. This was what he wanted to be: utterly free, almost naked, reclaiming the wild heritage of human beings as creatures of the jungle. Like Halycon Sage, he had been filled with horror at modern civilization—its dull coldness, its banality, its pointlessness. But now his time had come.

He had perfected his wild Tarzan-yell, blood-chilling to villains and invigorating to honest folk in trouble. He wanted to be a protector of the good, an avenger of wrongs. He had even tried swinging through the trees, giving it his best, but had realized before long that thick jungle vines were necessary. Thereafter, he had improvised a system of ropes but was still perfecting the technique. So far, his only achievement was a collection of bumps, bruises, and scratches from unsympathetic bark, along with a good assortment of blisters. The real Tarzan never used gloves.

CHAPTER
FOURTEEN

One day, Halycon Sage decided to look at the next seven rules from *How to Write a Novel*. For it must be confessed that, though he had gained some idea of the whole list from the introduction, he had only read the first three rules before becoming involved in one of those endless loops of complexity that were habitual with him.

Here they are.

<u>The Next Seven Rules</u>

4. Write about what you know. If you've grown up on a pig farm, don't try to write about Paris.
5. Write what is popular. No sense writing a book nobody will read!
6. Each character should have no more than three attributes. The first two should go together,

while the third should be contradictory, adding interest.

7. Describe characters and make them look different. If they *look* different enough, you won't have to bother making them think and talk differently!

8. Avoid characters with "other" genders, cultures, or ethnicities; you can't *really* know how they feel, now can you?

9. Research which agents and publishers accept what kinds of books. Write with them in mind.

10. Be spontaneous and authentic. Nobody likes a phony. And don't pay attention to rules.

Not too far away, someone very different was also engaged in an intellectual pursuit: the Shadowy Man was considering his grand idea. This magnificent idea was to replace everything positive, beautiful, kind, wise, honest, courageous, healthy, clear, truthful, or even sane with things that *seemed* very similar, but whose effect was the exact opposite. It could be done with art, with ambition, with friendship. The applications were endless!

Of course one could not attend to every detail; one had to find the fulcrum, the pivot point, or a number of them, which would affect everything else. These changes could be seeded here and there in subtle ways, unnoticeable until the whole climate of a society had changed. The town would never know what had hit it. And neither—and here he smiled a secret smile to himself—would Halycon Sage.

⁂

R uby had a habit of sleeping with her windows open. Even the screens were not always in place, for she had no fear of anything, animal or human, that might come in. Her reflexes were fast, she awoke instantly at any disturbance, and insects were minimal at this time of year in the high desert climate.

Thus it was that she awakened one night shortly after midnight—Sage was off somewhere—to find something . . . someone . . . determinedly chewing on her arm. In the dim light, the thing looked like maybe a raccoon or a badger, only that would have been terribly painful, wouldn't it? There was no pain, just an odd, unconvincing gnawing sensation, more like an itch, or an extremely inept massage.

She squinted at the furry thing covering her forearm. That was hair, *human* hair, medium brown, and the thing she saw there was the back of a messy-looking human head. The performance was unconvincing in the extreme, like a very bad actor trying to work himself up to playing a vampire. Oh . . .

"Now, really," said Ruby.

The Apocalypse Zombie raised his head, and their eyes met. "*Aghhroarrrawr,*" he moaned. Then, in a voice creaky from disuse, he added, "Had to try. Had to. It's part of my . . ."

"Job description," Ruby finished for him crisply.

There was nothing else to be said. Shambling and mumbling, the embarrassed Zombie made his exit through the bedroom door, knocking over small furnishings as he went, and stumbled awkwardly out the front door into the cool, starlit night.

CHAPTER

FIFTEEN

Introducing the Black Thread

In God there is a deep and dazzling darkness.
—William Blake[11]

Time to break cover, thought Layla, using an American idiom. Her English was good though slightly eccentric, and under the right circumstances, she had a lot to say for herself. But during the bad days after 9/11, she had learned to remain quiet while presenting a friendly yet unreadable face. It was just safer. And since she was a *hijabi*—a Muslim woman who covered her head and body in accordance with the dictates of her faith—perfect self-control was more important than it would have been for one less apt to become a target. Suddenly, the term "break cover" occurred to her in the new sense of taking off her hijab. While she certainly wasn't going to do *that*, the pun made her laugh. Besides concealing her good English and sensible, grounded intelligence, her impassive exterior concealed the fact that Layla had a decent sense of humor.

It's funny the way Abdurraheem is so sure he's the sensible one and I'm lost in a fog of religious clouds, thought Layla to herself. *Actually,* he's *the dreamer. Still trying to get ahead in the world, even though there's no more world to get ahead in, no competition, just everyone working together for survival. It's funny because he's a good man really, and everyone likes him. It's just that he has been scarred by the events of his life.* She offered up a brief prayer of thanks that, *inshallah,* their troubles were finally over.

The prejudice they had experienced and the diminution of their fortunes, from the prosperous family of a respected airline pilot to three homeless people sitting on a curb, had affected the two of them differently. While these challenges had made her more self-contained and more reliant on the Unseen, they had only redoubled his ambition to succeed now that he had been given a second chance.

Maybe he should start a political party with himself as the head of it. She shuddered. Corrupt politicians had almost destroyed everything. *Alhamdulillah,* thank God, they were gone now! Of course corrupt religion—one-sided, shallow, prejudiced, self-seeking religion—was every bit as bad. That was why she had to implement her plan: introduce some of the oddly assorted characters of Dry Creek Gulch to the *zikr*, the ancient Sufi Ceremony of Remembrance, which did not merely tell about Higher Reality but could take you there.

It was always necessary for one crew member to remain aboard the squidship, awake and alert, to make sure it didn't dissolve back into the imaginal world from which it had sprung. For it must be admitted that the Squid needed no ship—as we understand ships to be—but had manifested it solely for the convenience of the Earthers.

The same person would monitor bulletins from headquarters and broadcasts from inhabited planets and gas clouds. The junior crewsquid who usually got stuck with this job, previously mentioned as Seven, will henceforth be known as TechieSquid. He had not picked an Earth name as there had been no need; he was not going down. His Squidish designations would be neither pronounceable nor comprehensible to you who read this book.

His confinement to the ship made him a little bitter since, besides himself, only the zi were left behind, partying down in the Squidpool, though they claimed to be doing research. You may recall that the zi had been left on board lest their unfamiliarity shock the Earthers. Even Eleven, a zi officer who wore blue body make-up in public, had been assigned to the pool rather than the command deck.

While TechieSquid would rather have been down on the planet, he *was* discovering some half-way interesting things from the various broadcasts and other resources.

Meanwhile, Skull, erstwhile member of the Dirty Dog Gang, was reflecting that he had never really been *down* with the New World. He disliked the sickening sweetness and light of the new Canis Fidelis Grill and Juice Bar that had replaced his beloved Dirty Dog Bar. Sunlight streaming in through clean windows! What kind of crap was that for a respectable old biker bar? As we read in the Chronicle[12], "He missed the smoke and darkness of the old days, and the unidentifiable scum on the tables." He *still* missed them! He tried at times to sit in the last remaining dark corner and recapture the feeling, but it never really worked. The inexplicable absence of alcohol particularly annoyed him.

It might be true what people are saying, he thought, *and that puritanical windbag Halycon Sage is writing this whole mess and we're all trapped in it. Of course Sage wouldn't want any booze around. Everybody knows Indians can't hold their liquor—if he even is an Indian.* Skull didn't keep up with the gossip much, but he knew that there was some doubt about the matter, though the guy certainly looked Indian to *him*.

And how come a dude who'd mostly lost his memory was such a big cheese in this town anyway? Why did anybody listen to him? Him, his tough girlfriend, and his stupid horse. Or maybe Layla and Abdurraheem were writing it, with their crazy religion that forbids the stuff. Though some of the Muslims he'd known back in the war zone when he was a contractor had drank plenty!

His thoughts drifted back to Halycon Sage. It sounded pretty stupid that he might be writing this new world, but Skull would believe anything after some of the things he'd seen since the Event. Look at *that*, for instance. He glanced over at the other semi-dark space near the back of the bar where the Apocalypse Zombie lingered, trying to look as if he belonged there.

No wonder nobody talks to him. He's so ugly he's you-gly! In truth, it was the Zombie's shy air of alienation rather than his looks that was responsible for his isolation, but Skull did not know this.

Hmmm, thought Skull. *He seems like the kind of guy the Shadowy Dude was talking about. Maybe I'd better get to work.* He sidled over to the Zombie with a confidential air.

"Hey, Buddy, can I buy you . . . an apple juice?" Man, that just did not sound right! The Zombie grunted and started to move away.

"Hey, come on, I just wanna talk to ya." He laid a friendly hand on the Zombie's shoulder. It was a toss-up whether the Zombie would sit back down or punch him, but curiosity won out.

"What?" asked the Zombie foggily.

Editor's note: As Halycon Sage writes this on his clacking old typewriter, he is finding it irksome to keep typing "the Zombie," with the capital Z and all. He is also beginning to find the *sound* of it annoying. So, henceforward the Zombie will sometimes be called by his real name, which, unknown to anyone in town, is Edgar.

"Whaddaya want?" asked Edgar.

"You look like a guy that might appreciate a new opportunity."

"I do?"

Skull called to Emma, who happened to be the waitress on duty. "Two apples," he said, trying to sound cool over such a stupid order. Without acknowledging their relationship in any way, he handed her a small handful of dried beans in payment. She moved away with swishing hips. She was crazy about him. He knew she would still be waiting when he got bored and came looking for her. Right now, he had business to conduct.

"I know a guy. And I think he'd like to meet you. This committee crap ain't the only game in town."

"**H**ey, I know you're back there!" TechieSquid was irritable. He was doing a long shift on the ship by himself (for all practical purposes), and it was making him grumpy.

There was silence. The strangely-shaped creature was generally Squidly but also odd in several ways. It did not move. TechieSquid watched it. There was nothing else to do. After a while, the amorphous shape made a random movement, perhaps the Squid equivalent of a sneeze, or the scratching of an itch.

"Hah, gotcha!" said TechieSquid, taking the opportunity to practice some of his Earth idioms. "You might as well admit you're there."

Nothing. This creature was really weird, and after seeing it a few times, he had dubbed it MysterySquid. Though almost nothing from the Squid planet was without the characteristic luminescence[13], this creature was uniformly black, lacking any sparkle or shimmer, though there was a certain elegance to its black satin finish.

Equally strangely, MysterySquid refused to talk, or to communicate in any way. Finally, it was *shrimpy*—only about five feet tall. A wave of mild shock cascaded through the sleeping minds of the zi on the ship, causing TechieSquid to realize his mistake. As a telepath, you always had to be careful. At least making *The Prayer of Profound Apology to Our Brothers the Shrimp* would give him something to do till the rest of the crew got back.

CHAPTER

SIXTEEN

Halycon Sage was returning from one of his furtive trips to his bad-food stash when he took a wrong turn in the community's cold cave. Quite a while ago he had discovered the little hole at the far end of the area used by the townspeople, and also a correctly sized rock to plug it with.

One of the many funny things about Sage: he was scrupulously honest in big things, but in the little ones, not so much. While you could have trusted him with your newborn baby or your million dollars without a qualm, he was less reliable in these small matters. Thus, he snuck away to visit his baloney and Wonder Bread with no hesitation and little guilt. A man had to look out for himself, after all. No rationalization about it! Okay, well, maybe he did feel a little guilty for eating junk and avoiding work, but he did it anyway.

Occupied with these and other thoughts, Sage turned wrong, then turned wrong again. Now, he was in a part of the cave that had barely been explored.

There was nothing interesting back there according to the preliminary investigation, and there was little time in the new world for superfluous side activities that did not directly contribute to group survival.

He paused, realizing he had lost his way. There was a long, blank wall on his left. But he felt something was here, something for *him*. While his earthly senses sometimes tuned in and out, his mystical sense was unerring. He was a fox hound, ever alert for the scent of some revelation or cosmic weirdness. There was indeed something here. He calmed himself, slowed his breath, and looked at the wall. Expecting nothing in particular, he waited patiently.

His patience was rewarded. Slowly, gradually, fiery letters began to appear on the wall. They looked like the Tolkien runes representing the Elvish language. (Sage had been dipping into *The Fellowship of the Ring*[14], a treasure he had found in the back of the Dirty Dog. Surprisingly, he had never read it.)

And yes, Dear Reader, it is contradictory to say that no one had any spare time for superfluous things while also saying that Halycon Sage was both reading and writing. But then that was Halycon Sage, still essentially a man of mystery. And while some might believe these activities represented a mere lazy shirking on his part, those who know him best know that his instinctive treasure hunts for God-knows-what sometimes yield surprising results.

The letters had solidified now. They were fiery in the sense that their shapes were flame-like, but their glow was gentle. Leaning a little forward he read,

Magic Theatre. For madmen only.
Price of admission: your mind[15].

Well, I paid that long ago, he thought, and continued watching the wall to see if anything else would turn up.

In one of those coincidences that happen more often than we realize, Ratbone, at this very moment, was reading *The Fellowship of the Ring* to Nuri. Sage had left his copy carelessly in the kitchen area of the Dog, and Ratbone had picked it up, thinking it looked interesting. He had never read it either. Since Nuri was almost six—ready to attend the town's makeshift school—Ratbone thought it was high time to introduce him to good literature. The fact that Nuri still sucked his thumb and seemed unusually small for his age was one more reason to help his development along in every way possible. Ratbone had had a rough childhood and even though the conditions here and now were about as different as could be imagined, he did not believe the survivalist jungle that was school would have changed all that much.

It was evening, and he was reading Nuri his bedtime story. Layla and Abdurraheem were busy—she was engaged in a cooking project, while he was finishing the blueprints for the glider he was building.

Ratbone realized it wasn't necessary for the kid to understand every word, only that he become absorbed in the rhythm of the story. This was good since they were reading the section where Tom Bombadil recites poetry to his ponies, a section that could be tough going for a five-year-old. In this way they were alike: Both had a love for words-as-music, possibly born of their experiences with funk, jazz, and rap on the one hand and the ancient languages of Arabic and Farsi on the other. While Preisczech shared their propensity to make little jingles out of everything, Ratbone considered Preisczech's natural aesthetic sense inferior to Nuri's.

So Ratbone read, delighting in the rhythms to which his varied life had sensitized him, adjusting his reading to make the beats come out right:

Hey! now! Come hoy now! Whither do you wander?
Up, down, near or far, here, there or yonder?
Sharp-ears, Wise-nose, Swish-tail and Bumpkin,
White-socks my little lad, and old Fatty Lumpkin!

He had already read the whole poem to Nuri once, but somehow it was this verse that brought the greatest delight to them both. Nuri began bouncing beside Ratbone like a much younger child. "Old Fatty Lumpkin," he chanted, laughing. "Old Fatty Lumpkin!"

At this moment, the still-anonymous orange cat walked up on his soft, noiseless paws and looked at Nuri inquiringly. His clear green eyes, the color of a peridot, were full of mystery, full of secrets and ancient knowledge. "Old Fatty Lumpkin," repeated Nuri, more solemnly, in an almost ceremonial manner.

"That's it!" said Ratbone. "He bees Fatty Lumpkin alright."

Though his whitish tummy exhibited a pleasing roundness at times, the hitherto anonymous orange cat was neither fat, nor old, nor lumpy. Yet he accepted the name.

Fatty Lumpkin stepped delicately onto Nuri's lap, assumed a curled position, and began to purr.

Another cave. A different one, high in the mountains. As different from the cave of Halycon Sage as could be imagined, not in geographical configuration, but in aim, purpose, and atmosphere. Only the elite were allowed here, the elect, not the ordinary run of useless peasants, the human cattle whose sole purpose was to be manipulated. *Well,* thought the Shadowy Man, scrupulously correcting himself, *perhaps that was not entirely true. Because there were also human tools, stooges to be used and thrown away.* These too were sometimes brought here, being necessary to his plan. On this day, they too were invited.

Ratbone was gradually realizing he would have to face something he'd been doing his best to avoid.

It was this: there was something just not right about Nuri. And if he, August Rathbone, was the only one who noticed, then the responsibility for saying something was his alone. As bright as the child obviously was, he was supposed to be turning six in a couple of months, and no six year-old on Earth had ever acted the way Nuri did.

Ratbone considered. Maybe it was just that he himself was used to tough city kids. Or maybe foreign kids were different. But look at the way the child had acted around the whole cuttlefish situation. And the bouncing and giggling and sucking his thumb. No. No way. Ratbone shook his head and abruptly decided. He would have to talk to the parents. Because they did not appear to notice that anything was wrong.

CHAPTER
SEVENTEEN

Layla was nervous. This was the first time she had gathered the group for the Sufi Ceremony of Divine Remembrance. *Seven-thirty after supper*, the directions had said. Her house. *Come one-by-one, come alone, come quietly. Enter by the side door.* To stay away from the kitchen and bedroom at the opposite ends of the house where Abdurraheem might be found.

She was not really going behind his back with this plan. He was so absorbed in his own work that he spent little time asking what she was doing or thinking about. He would not exactly have disapproved, but he would have found her new venture odd and pointless. In any case, she would have to tell him eventually. There was no point in disturbing him now.

"Come in," said Layla to her first guest. The experience reminded Preisczech of stories he'd heard from his home country's Communist days, of people slipping in twos and threes through the dark woods to attend forbidden Christian meetings[16].

Preisczech was perhaps the most surprising person Layla had invited to her gathering. He was purely scientific with no interest in religion of any kind, but she had included him out of a feeling that he might be lonely, with Jenny so busy and Sage often away on mysterious business. Preisczech noticed that Layla had abandoned her usual black in favor of a long white dress and head covering.

By 8 p.m. everyone was there. She had welcomed them graciously and offered them delicious home-made baklava and strong coffee. Don't ask how she managed this post Event—women have their mysterious ways. Now they were seated in a circle, the room illuminated by candles.

The group was an odd assortment. Besides Layla and Preisczech, the circle included Nuri, Ratbone, a few innocuous townsfolk, and four Squid. On a last-minute impulse, Layla had also asked Emma, that baker of delicious cookies who always hung back a little in every group.

Ratbone had been invited as the only neighbor Layla knew with a definite interest in religion, though as with everything else, he viewed it from his own peculiar angle. (In their notes about this later, the Squid assumed that Ratbone had been included for his *color*, since the Earthers designated him as Black, and Layla's *zikr* was obviously a Black Thread Activity.) Halycon Sage had been a possibility, but as she understood neither his books nor his motivations, she had decided to wait. Maybe later.

The four Squidly guests had been invited because of their names. Mohammed Schmidt, Muhammad Wang Smith, Obiwan Mohammed, and Lol-Bey were obviously Muslims and should be included, unless and until they exhibited Wahabi/Salafi extremist tendencies. Layla was nervous about this. Were there fundamentalist Squid?

Of course the whole fundamentalist designation was ridiculous since many of those so labelled fundamentally violated the religion with every breath. Never mind. It had been necessary to invite these Squid, she had been pleased to invite them, and they appeared pleased to be there.

They had not partaken of pastry or coffee and they did not sit, but stood respectfully around the table, appearing to delight in the peaceful atmosphere and the electrical air of expectation. It was time to start.

Sheep skins were placed in a circle on the floor like small, individual rugs, creamy white, with a single deep blue one where the leader would sit. In the center stood a vase-shaped drum and, on a low table, a burning candle. Layla assumed the leader's position, inviting her guests with a gentle gesture to take their places around the circle.

"Welcome," she said, a little shyly, but with dignity too. "This is something new to you, but very old, practiced for over a thousand years in many countries. This is the *zikrullah*, the Ceremony of Divine Remembrance." She gave it the simpler pronunciation, easier for speakers of English.

"We will sit, then stand, and sing the ancient words as we move in rhythm. Our tradition says that *zikr* removes the rust from the mirror of the heart. It is holy. Sacred. It is from the Muslims, but here in this safe place, it can be for everybody."

Layla stopped, feeling she had said enough, possibly *too* much. She raised her hands and called the *Fatiha*, the Prayer of Opening, translations of which convey so little of what is really there. Then she began to chant, first giving the English meanings in simple words, then inviting her guests to join in repeating the Arabic phrases. A grounding was established. Leaving them to maintain the low-voiced chanting, she moved upwards through a musical scale they did not know. Ratbone thought of the subtle light of dawn and twilight. It sounded like that.

Next came a sonorous hum, filling the room like fragrance. A more complex melody was added, mid-range and higher tones bringing texture to the landscape of sound. Suddenly, there was a ringing like crystal in the air, coming from everywhere and nowhere.

Who's making the harmonics? Ratbone wondered. It couldn't be Layla. She was busy with the melody. He looked around. The Squid were doing it. Apart from everything else, it appeared that the Squid could sing. *And* damn *they can sing,* he thought, shaking his head.

There was something of the feel of whale song. Not only from the Squid, though, from everyone, and from the air itself. The circle swayed gently, like reeds in a river. The drum came in, a subtle, rhythmic beat, a whiff of Africa, almost. *No,* thought Ratbone, *Baghdad and Najaf, Stamboul and Isfahan . . . Ancient names.*

He looked at Layla. Her eyes were closed, her face transformed. Touching the drum, she sang the complex melody line, voice flowing over the rhythm with clarity, a quiet passion. The Squid responded, increasing their intensity, and others followed. Something strange was happening, as though some ordinary doors of perception had closed, while unsuspected ones were opening.

Emma could not say how long the ceremony lasted or even exactly what was happening. Swaying, chanting, prayer, music. Light and color. At some point, they stood. Sometimes they linked hands. She was not exactly awake, but certainly not dreaming. This was something new. She released the need to understand, riding on the waves of sound, tears flowing down her cheeks, unnoticed. She was not the only one weeping, and over on one side, someone else was laughing hugely. The tears and the laughter were both acceptable and added depth to the music.

Preisczech thought, *Layla's wrong, this is not new to me at all. I have always known this.* Then the timeless time was over. An hour? Three hours? He had no idea.

Layla ended with a prayer, first in Arabic, then in English. She thought her guests might like it, and that it would be good for them.

Oh, Beloved God, Opener of the Gates of Prosperity,
And the Gates of Happiness, and the Gates of Mercy,
And the Gates of Utmost Compassion and Love,

And the Gates of Nourishment, and the Gates of
Pure Life,
And the Gates of Security and the Gates of Well-
Being,
And the Gates of Peace.
Oh Opener! Oh Revealer! Oh Opener! Oh God, open
for us the Best
and Most Sublime of Your Gates!

Ya FaTAhu, ya FaTAhu, ya FaTAh! Ya Allah, iftah
lana khayr-ul-Bab.

So, it was true then, what they had felt. New and unaccustomed doors *were* opening within them. Layla, for her part, was glad that nobody in the room had the common American name of Bob. Since the Arabic word for door or gate sounds much like that name, the hypothetical Bob might have been embarrassed[17].

Later, the joyful Squid went home, their light fed and replenished at last. They were assured that at least the Black Thread part of their plan for the Earthers had succeeded, that seeds of a new, harmonious era had been safely planted and were beginning to grow. The fact that at least one woman and her small group understood how beings should be fed—with light, motion, tone, and rhythm, beautiful in sound and effect, rather than with hunks of physical matter—was vastly encouraging.

Only Lol-Bey, most junior of those present, stayed behind. During a moment when everyone else was absorbed in the deep bliss of the zikr, he had happened to open his eyes and glance around. He had seen Nuri's orange cat rushing backwards over the hardwood floor. Fascinated, he watched the actions of this other type of alien creature, wondering if he played some part in the ritual. The cat was making strange sounds and stopping periodically, as though depositing some precious substance at certain, predetermined intervals. He did not begin leaving deposits until he had reached the large area of colorful material the humans referred to as a "carpet."

After the zikr, Lol-Bey slithered forward and examined what the cat had left behind. Ah. He obtained the necessary materials and wiped up the clear, gluey cat vomit, which would otherwise be coldly unpleasant on the tentacles come morning. And, remembering his manners and the obligatory rituals of his own people, he intoned, "Thank you, honest paper towel. Your life was not in vain. You died in a noble cause."

Lol-Bey took several days to contemplate his observations of the second alien species, the orange strip-ed one. Perhaps he had been hasty in assuming the deposits regurgitated by the cat were merely the result of an upset stomach. The creature was too intelligent and subtle to perform an action, especially in the middle of a vital ceremony, that did not have multiple meanings.

Thinking deeply, Lol-Bey realized that the second meaning was one of rejection, expelling that which was unhealthy and wrong. There was a wrongness somewhere that must be expelled. So far, so good. The wrongness could not be connected with the zikr, which resonated with the deep rightness of the Black Thread. He must seek elsewhere.

He sent out his mind's antennae, subtle inquiring threads like hair-thin filaments of light. There was the village, bent on survival and stabilization. The village was good. There was a cave: strange and unprecedented, full of time and space anomalies, but also good. He must seek further.

Scanning . . . scanning . . .

Ah. There was another cave, and the wrongness emanated from that place, and from one being within it. Perhaps at some point, he would need to go there.

CHAPTER
EIGHTEEN

n the second cave, the one whose emanation of wrongness had been felt by Lol-Bey, the Shadowy Man was speaking to his motley and ill-assorted audience of scruffy humans, one really peculiar-looking character whom Skull had brought along, and a couple of Squid.

"We live for art, you see, as there is nothing else. Imploded concepts, such as truth, god, meaning, kindness, personal responsibility, all have been proven absurd. Discarded by the best minds. Art alone remains."

He took a sip from his brandy glass.

"I like art," ventured the odd-looking one vaguely. "I like beauty. Because it makes me happy." His voice sounded creaky and unused.

The Shadowy Man exploded with laughter.

"Ah, my naive young friend. Beauty. Happiness." He chuckled again. "Equally outmoded and ridiculous ideas, representing exactly *nothing* in the real world. But you will learn better, young man. You're lucky you came to me and not to those fools in the valley. You will learn better. And if you are very lucky, you will be one of the wise, the elect. Those chosen by a meaningless fate. We face reality, cold, hard, and brutal as it is. That is our strength and our glory. Regard this."

He stepped to where a sheet covered part of the cave wall and drew it back. Behind it was a painting, sort of. It was a skeleton, and it was on fire. It was rendered in vomitous green, maggot white, and dull black. The bones were out of drawing, badly proportioned. Some incomprehensible blue slashes crossed it diagonally at random points. There was a splash of red across the middle that could have indicated blood or merely a moment of petulant paint-throwing by the artist. Where the eyes would have been were a shriveled plum and a giant raspberry.

"There," said the Shadowy Man. "Where is your beauty *now*?"

In other developing disasters:
"Commander, I think you'd better see this," said TechieSquid. Silently, he handed Commander Kennedy his report, which included transcripts, originally paper, but now preserved in small blue cubes. The first was a list of Squidish cultural attributes, evidently created by some Earthean scientific researcher, though informally presented. The second was an article from a minor newsletter or specialty paper entitled *Squidly Times* and purporting

to be written by grammarians and linguists. Obviously, anything like this was of the utmost importance!

Both papers were from the near future. One was from True Earth, the other from the Alternate Universe. They dealt with the same incident, now code-named "Barbecue," and said incident was profoundly disturbing.

Though the Dirty Dog Gang no longer existed, some signs of it remained: former members in the town, others up in the hills, and the way in which many people still referred to the town's only restaurant and community headquarters inappropriately as the Dirty Dog Bar. Emma, sometime waitress and occasional manager, was wiping tables in preparation for closing, pushing her honey-blonde hair back from her forehead. *Jeez, it's hot in here!* she thought. She was also thinking about her boyfriend, Skull, and she made a little sound of dissatisfaction.

Back when they'd rode with the gang, things had been different, though he had never been kind or even very interested in her. She'd had the other Dogs and a few random ladies to hang out with, so she was never lonely, and like the rest of them, she loved motorcycles and felt comfortable in the bar.

Now it was different. Everything had changed and he had left her alone, heading into the mountains with Wolf and a bunch of would-be mountain men, playing his stupid macho games. He came down occasionally, but big deal. Even when he was here, he was cool and dismissive, and she had started to notice little things about him, like his general failure to wash.

Emma felt shy because she knew everyone thought she was stupid. In the early, chaotic days when life was harder and people needed a laugh, Skull had shared her little mishap with the wooden cutting board far and wide, making her a laughingstock.

She'd been so excited about learning to cook and bake from Jenny! While her own mother had relied on the freezer and the microwave, Emma was sure she could make something delicious if she only had half a chance.

Not wanting to spoil her cookies with onion and garlic flavors, she'd had the idea of carving initials on the two sides of the cutting board so she could tell them apart. She was skilled at carving letters, having been taught by her father before he took off, and she was proud of the fact that she knew the word savory, something picked up from a magazine. She worked hard at the little project in her very limited spare time, angling the insides of the letters and finishing the result with fine sandpaper. Unfortunately, caught up in the elegant curves of the S, she forgot that sweet and savory started with the same letter, making her project silly and useless.

When she showed the cutting board to Skull, raising and turning it shyly but with pardonable pride, he had roared with laughter, then spent the next week telling everyone he knew. She had moved on. But a slight sense of betrayal and injury remained, as did a certain reserve in reaching out to others or sharing her thoughts. She *was* becoming a good cook and baker, everyone acknowledged that! But still. *Being lonely really sucks. If things were different, maybe it could be fun here.*

Her eye was drawn by a slight movement in the corner of the room. That one corner was always kind of dark, and sometimes a second corner was dark as well, though sometimes not. This was one of several strange things about the Cannes Fidelis Grill and Juice Bar. Now, she could almost swear she saw a kind of octopus thing moving in the corner. Well, not an octopus exactly, but sort of. The general shape and the legs were different. She looked again, but the motion had stopped and the thing, whatever it was, seemed to be trying to blend into the darkness.

It was well equipped for such a task, being uniformly black. Emma wondered if it was one of these Squid that people kept talking about—she hadn't paid much attention. They were supposed to be aliens from space who had been insulted somehow at a dinner and gone off in a huff. She wasn't sure she believed any of it and had not followed the discussion closely. *Anyway, if this is the same thing, they sure described it all wrong!* This one was barely five feet tall, forget eight or ten, and it had no blue or green on it and certainly no sparkles. Probably just people trying to make things sound more exciting, as usual.

Suddenly, she had the oddest feeling that the thing was talking to her. She heard calm words in a soothing female voice. *Don't worry, Doll, sometimes they act like that. You don't have to put up with it. You don't have to stay with that jerk. You can have a life. We're here for you.*

Who's we? There was only one Squid Lady there, if that was what it was. *Maybe I'm just losing my mind. That might make things go better.* But now she saw that there were two of them. The other was quite different, indeed and truly eight or nine feet tall, colored a deep and shimmering blue, and with more sparkles than a best-selling vampire novel.

Yes, we'll be here for you, said the second one, the big sparkly one. It was sort of majestic, and like the first speaker, it felt and sounded female. *This is Emma,* said the sparkly one, introducing her to the small, black Squid. *You'll like her.*

I wonder why she's introducing me as if she already knows me. She nodded once in polite greeting and closed her eyes happily. When she opened them again, the strange beings were gone, but that didn't matter. Being part of some sisterhood from outer space was *way* more important than messing up a stupid cutting board and a lot cooler than running around the mountains playing army.

⁐

"**S**age?" inquired Ruby, somewhat tentatively one day.

"What?" he replied, abstracted. He was writing.

124

"If you wanted to write something different, something a bit more modern, I wouldn't object. It might make the books more popular."

"You mean I might get a third reader instead of just two critics?"

"Well, it could help. Using three stars every time the lights go out is a little old fashioned."

Sage was startled. This did not sound like Ruby. Her dark hair, for once unbound from its braid, swept tantalizingly over her bare shoulders. He realized again how beautiful she was. The fine chiffon of her nightdress lay like a gauzy galaxy across the firmament of her breasts. He felt his breath quicken.

"If you wanted to, you could write about *us*. You know, change the names."

There was a timeless pause while he considered this idea.

"No," said Halycon Sage and pulled down the shades.

Editor's Note: This really, really does *not* sound like Ruby! It is quite possible that, as happened sometimes in the previous Chronicle (e.g., vampire novel), Halycon Sage was attempting a new genre but quickly thought better of it.

A short distance away, Ratbone was facing his own difficulties.

Oh, man, I'd rather be anywhere but here. Abdurabeem's still stuck on his status, even though they ain't no status no more. And I'm gonna tell him his kid is subnormal? This is not *gonna go well.* He hastily corrected the "subnormal" in his mind. Nuri was a beautiful kid—intelligent, kind, intuitive, with a sort of sparkle about him. He was a great little kid, but that was the problem. He was a *little* kid, more like a brilliant toddler than an almost-six-year-old.

Maybe he should have approached Layla, but even after the powerful zikr, her quietness scared him. She was dignified and, like her son, kind. But she wore that black thing and presented a peaceful face that revealed almost nothing. He had no idea what was going on beneath her calm exterior. So he knocked on the garage workshop door, ready to face the proud, ambitious, and possibly touchy father on this, a most sensitive subject.

Abdurraheem turned from the schematic of his glider, which he had been tweaking. He strongly disliked being interrupted, but he would never forget how Ratbone and Wolf had come to the aid of his family in their darkest hour. Abdurraheem always had a smile for this man, who had also befriended his son and sometimes took care of him when the other adults were busy.

"Muhammad, my man, let me run it down to you," said Ratbone, trying and failing to appear at his ease. "Your Nuri ain't normal. He's a great kid, but there's somethin' a little off. He ain't playin' with a full deck."

There. It was out. Not very tactful, perhaps, but better than beating around the bush.

Abdurraheem appeared frozen. He stood over the sink, facing away so that Ratbone could not see his expression.

"And why do you think this? The boy is alert, intelligent, friendly, lively."

"Well yeah," said Ratbone, "but he does a lot of stuff that's just not age appropriate."

Most of the tension seemed to go out of Abdurraheem's shoulders. He turned slightly toward Ratbone.

"Like what?" he asked.

Suddenly Ratbone was worried that this dad would just blow the whole thing off, decide it was nothing. And it *wasn't* nothing, it was important! Ratbone could feel the wrongness in the kid's behavior, and, okay, he could admit it: he loved Nuri. There hadn't been no little kids in his life for a long, long time, and this one was wonderful. Long before his Fifth Street Mofo days, he'd spent some time around an idealistic inner-city preschool program, and he had a feeling for how kids should be at different ages. Desperate to communicate, he slowed, calmed, got a grip on himself.

"Okay, I'll give you an example. I was reading to him the other day, and I read him this little poem, see, out of *Fellowship of the Ring*, and he really liked it. We both did, we like the rhythm. But he starts bouncing up and down repeating it like a little kid. He does stuff like that all the time. He puts his head on my knee and falls asleep! He's almost six, he should be ready for school! He acts like he's four!"

The father turned toward his friend. He was smiling. "My dear Mr. Rathbone, I'm so sorry to have deceived you. It was necessary at one time, and then it was difficult to explain . . . I didn't think it mattered here, now, in this new world we're in.

"You see, there was a private school in California where we lived. It took only the most promising, the most intelligent children, and there was an age minimum. Very expensive, but it would have ensured his future. Now, of course . . ." He stopped a moment, running his fingers through his hair. "My friend, we lied to you, we lied to everybody."

Ratbone stared at him, frozen in suspense.

"Nuri *is* four," said the father. "In fact, he hasn't even really been four all that long."

He was about to offer further explanations, but Ratbone was out the door, laughing, waving his big bass-player's hand in parting.

"Say no more, my man. Say no more." He was relieved beyond measure. And then he had another thought. He stopped, frozen in his tracks, "Oh, Jah Love!" he said, speaking out loud in his shocked and laughing bemusement. "Another f'ing genius!"

Attention, humans. Though this novel appears to be all in fun, there are important messages being transmitted to you though its pages. You would be well advised to heed them. This has been a public service message.
—F. Atty. Lumpkin, Esq. (a.k.a. Fatty Lumpkin)

CHAPTER
NINETEEN

It was evident that Sophie or one of her colleagues had found a cultural informant among the Squid themselves. Just who this was we are not at this moment prepared to disclose. — The Editors

A Guide to the Squidren
Vol. 2
for the Edification, Preparation,
and Information
of the Remaining World Civilization
by Sophie MacGregor et al.

We have more information for you—included, as always, in the order in which it was discovered (mostly).

1. The Squid are very ceremonial in their approach to life, and their religion is very important to them. While this religion in many ways agrees

with the deepest mystical teachings of Earth, it has some odd features.

2. The Squid, while not prone to physical violence, are extremely contentious about things that matter to them.

3. During the Choosing of Names that occurred on the Squidship (though no such ceremony had existed before their approach to Earth), an extremely serious argument broke out between the Squidren who insisted that a popular Earth Name should be spelled "Muhammad" and those who defended the spelling "Mohammed" with equal fervor. The resulting breakdown in unity almost caused the Squidren to turn their ship around and go home, abandoning the entire project (see 1 and 2, above).

4. A historic precedent can be found in the serious and ongoing disagreement between those Squidren who call their holy book *The Book of Lighted Squid* and the somewhat historically later contingent who refer to it as *The Book of Squidly Light*. Both groups call themselves LightSQUIDians and dispute the right of the other group to do so. The importance of this disagreement cannot be overestimated. We, the present authors, were surprised to learn that members of both groups were together in the same ship!

❦

One day, while contemplating the cave wall, Halycon Sage had a strange vision. Like an old television gradually tuning in, there were lines and fuzz and squiggles and then suddenly, there was the face of Ratbone, large and emphatic-looking.

"Hey y'all, humans! Yeah, you! Listen up." He gazed out at a crowd of amorphous onlookers with the fierce, determined look of an effective middle school teacher. He began to pace. "Now, I'm gonna divide you into two groups. Half of you gonna stand over there, the other half here." He indicated opposite ends of the underground chamber where Halycon Sage's special wall was located.

"Don't move *yet!* Okay, we gonna divide up based on your answers to some questions. Would you like to save the Earth from being destroyed? The oceans and forests and dolphins and puppies 'n stuff? Do you think you shouldn't hurt people you've never met, like, blow them up or set them on fire? Do you think food and water should be distributed fairly so nobody dies 'cause they don't have any? Okay, you cats go there.

"A few more questions. Do you think it doesn't matter what you do as long as you make a lot of money? Do you think *your* people are way better than any other people? Do you think those other people aren't even really people at all and it would be better to just kill them? Okay, y'all go over there." He indicated the opposite end of the chamber, then addressed his remote viewing audience (only Halycon Sage at the moment) and said impressively, "These are the only sides *there are*, and the only sides *there ever were or will be*. This has been a public service announcement."

Since the new post-Event world had no major group rivalries (except on the Food committee), no bombs or incendiary weapons, and almost no people, Halycon Sage was hard put to understand what Ratbone was talking about. Also, "Um, Teacher?" inquired Sage politely, tentatively raising his hand from his bent elbow.

The Ratbone image on the wall sighed with a slightly exaggerated patience. "Yes?"

"What about the people in the middle? You know, draftees and young guys who want to serve their . . ."

"Got it!" said Ratbone. "Okay, who thinks you want to serve your community and your leaders know better than you do, so if they tell you to go kill some bad guys, then those guys are bad and you should kill them?" There was a pause while some tentative hands within the phantom audience went up.

"Okay, y'all are in the middle. But what I want you to remember: don't ever pick sides based on your religion or your nationality or your color or any of that stuff. Because that stuff is just pure, one hundred percent *granfaloon*[18]! It don't have nothin' to do with the real sides. The real sides are the ones I just ran down to you and, yeah, the group in the middle."

There was something wrong with this. Halycon Sage raised his hand again with the question that really mattered. If he'd been a for-sure Indian instead of whatever he actually *was*—and this was part of what his amnesia had obscured, though the look of his face and body and some of his cultural assumptions seemed pretty definitive—it would have been his *first* question.

"So what if you die fighting to protect your people? What if somebody really *is* trying to wipe out your culture and everyone you know?"

"You got me," said Ratbone, lifting his hands in a surrendering gesture. "Those people go to the highest heaven. The *highest* heaven. Because they give everything."

Ratbone's face faded out and a little sign appeared on the wall, written in the cool, fiery letters surrounded by old-fashioned scrollwork. It read:

"Thank you, Mr. Augustus Rathbone. To our audience: The opinions of the previous speaker do not necessarily reflect the Book of Lighted Squid, the Squidiler assigned to the Cave Wall Project, or the Squidren as a whole. Thanks for watching, Halycon Sage. Kwaheri!"

Man, thought Ratbone, taking in the approaching dawn and stretching his long arms and legs out of his bed to greet the day. *That was one crazy dream. Musta been the* zikr.

At their camp, Skull was addressing the Troop. Somewhat against their better judgment, Rap and Wolf had given him the floor. This nightly time around the campfire was the chance for everyone to say their piece.

"So, why are we out here?" asked Skull dramatically. The answers were more varied than he expected.

"Because it's beautiful."

"'Cause now's our chance to live free, the way we always wanted."

"'Cause the people in the town are a bunch of dinks, and I don't wanna work that hard."

"Right!" said Skull, focusing on the last two comments while ignoring the incomprehensible beauty stuff, which seemed to keep cropping up. He figured it must be the desert night with its billion stars that had everybody going so soft. He shook himself back into focus.

"Right! We don't wanna obey their stupid rules and spend all our time fetching and carrying and working on stupid committees. We wanta live free. FREE!"

Everybody dutifully roared, "FREE!" in response.

Wolf and Rap exchanged a look of understanding. Some of these dudes were not that smart, but you had to let them have their say. Couldn't just tell them to shut up, tempting though it might be. "Well, I know a guy who can make us even FREE-ER!"

"FREE-ER!" they all roared, and after that, it was a piece of cake.

A few days after the strange vision or dream shared by Halycon Sage and Ratbone, there were the fiery letters on the cave wall again, fine and flame-shaped. Sage looked at them.

Here is the truth.

Everything you experience is illusory, and everything you experience is real. It is real, but it is not what it appears to be to <u>you</u>. A fly (small earth creature) sees everything splintered into thousands of facets. Is that the reality of things or only the fly's eye view? But the fly's eye view is also true.

Everything is in layers and levels, and sometimes they appear to contradict one another. Your life is a journey through them. You are travelling a path. If you wish it, a <u>glorious</u> path.

There is meaning everywhere.

There is meaning in everything.

Ultimate reality is a Who, not a What, and while you do not wholly comprehend this and never well, you are not separate from It by so much as the width of an eyelash.

What you read here is not Ultimate Truth but is carefully calibrated to your individual state and station, your momentarily expanded awareness and your default setting at this point in your journey.

Thanks for listening, Halycon Sage. We hope this was helpful to you. Kwaheri!

—The Book of Lighted Squid

A Chinese puzzle. Boxes within boxes within boxes. Realizing how much he had in common with them, Halycon Sage also realized he was in some danger of becoming a LightSQUIDian.

A Guide to the Squidren
Vol. 3
For the Edification, Preparation,
and Information
of the Remaining World Civilization
by Sophie MacGregor et al.

1. Again, followers of *The Book of Lighted Squid* are called "LightSQUIDians," with the emphasis on the second syllable.

2. Seems trivial but is not: the word Squid is almost *always* capitalized. Duels have been fought over this. The one exception: in compound nouns, such as squidpants, no capital is used. However, this does not seem to apply to *all* compound nouns.

   Colleague's Note: I'm sorry, the capitalization of compound words seems to be completely random. I have seen "squidship," "SquidShip," and "Squidship"!

3. While a small group of Squid without a particular purpose, a *granfaloon*, so to speak, are called by their collective noun, Squidiler,

if they have come together with a definite aim they are known as a squidsquad (note again the incomprehensible absence of capitalization in the compound noun).

Colleague's Note: This can't be right! Because our group of Squid officers here on Earth <u>always</u> refer to themselves in plural as Squidiler, and they certainly have a definite aim!

Response: Alright, keep your shirt on, you don't learn all the rules of a language in a day! I <u>said</u> in Vol. 1 that these rules for plurals were not reliable! –Sophie

4. Similarly, a group of twelve or more Squid are called Squidren, but if they are assembled for a specific purpose and acting as a unit, they may also be referred to as *a* Squidren.

5. Trouble has developed on Earth because some yahoos decided that Lighted Squid had something to do with *barbecue*. While the Squidiler in question were rescued without harm except for the shock to their feelings, this barbarous reaction has contributed to the unwarranted conclusion, accepted by weak minds, that the term Lighted Squid should be avoided entirely and the Holy Book referred to as *The Book of Squidly Light*.

Note from Sophie: I think we'll have to rewrite number five. It seems to be mainly a product of wild rumors and cultural bias.

6. Shocking news flash! The Squid did not really need a spaceship at all. They swim naturally through time and space as easily as through air or ocean water. The ship is purely for our comfort, manifested to make humans feel at home since, if aliens *did* come, we were expecting them to show up in a spaceship.

PART THREE

THE BARBECUE

*WHEREIN the Red Thread is unveiled and illumined.
In this case, action is required!*

CHAPTER
TWENTY

wo strangers had wandered into the Troop's camp and had been there for several days; this was weird, though not unheard of. There were still a few wild characters crawling out of the cracks among the foothills and mountains. Rap instantly dubbed these two clowns "Stetson Black" and "Spiffy".

Stetson Black, wearing the stereotypical western villain's hat, was the leader, and something about him made Rap's spine tingle unpleasantly. Spiffy was the sidekick, too well-dressed for the desert. He tried to talk like the rest of the Troop, but his dialogue kept slipping. He was a constant complainer about everything, especially the food. Beaner, watching an interaction around the campfire, predicted that it wouldn't be long till Rap and Wolf politely asked the visitors to leave (or not so politely if they didn't take the hint).

"I'm sick of eating the same old crap," complained Spiffy.

"What, you don't like rabbit, bugs, wild onions?" asked Skull, whose extreme thinness seemed at odds with his tendency to scarf down every morsel in sight. "You a picky eater?"

"This food is disgusting! All that *fish!* And is trout the only fish in the stream? Can we not have something different?" His normal, western accent had slipped into some funny kind of British.

Rap shook his head. This guy was crazy. There was no better food in the world than brook trout right out of the water. Must be some rich kid because he'd obviously never had to last for months on cans of beans and packets of ramen.

"And the *cooking method!*" the guy went on. Yup. A rich kid. "Everything into the frying pan. Have you no imagination?"

Beaner stared, wondering how the speaker, annoying as he was, had managed to keep his teeth and nose unbroken in the fairly rough environment of the camp. Though guns were long gone and the group got along better than might have been expected, there were still plenty of fights, especially when people played the fool. But *this* guy looked like an actor right off a set, perfect complexion, no black eye, not even a sunburn.

A shill, thought Rap. *This is some kind of set up.* His analysis was essentially correct, but the thought passed through his head and out the other side, so to speak. *There are no con games in this new world, only bare survival,* he thought. *The con games will come later.*

Suddenly, Spiffy changed the mood, looking around triumphantly as though he'd had a new idea. "Hey, how about some barbecue? I saw some sauce in one of the houses down there. Maybe it's still around. We could go get it. And charcoal and stuff."

"Hey, that's a good idea!" exclaimed Skull.

Like clockwork, the conversation was proceeding from one premise to the next. Rap, who had been a hip-hop and spoken word artist and done a bit of acting, had the sense that the exchanges were scripted with some particular aim in mind, though what it was he could not imagine. But he had one fault, probably the reason that, with all his skills, he had never risen higher in life than being Ratbone's number two man in the Fifth Street Mofos. He would always second guess himself.

Intuition and quick instincts are equally necessary in the inner city and in the wild, and trusting them could be the difference between life and death. *But . . . Nah,* thought Rap, *I'm imagining stuff again.* And he tuned out the discussion, wondering in a vague way whether he could find a hot spring in the hills or the nearby desert. Sitting in hot water again would be tight. He got up and wandered away.

Obiwan Mohammed was a shy and unassuming Squid, small in stature, though not positively stunted like MysterySquid. She was retiring in

character and calm in demeanor. It was possible that she would become the first great Squidly author to be acknowledged on Earth, proving that those who say little may be thinking all the more. But that was many years in the future and only occurred in about half of the possible timelines. In the others, her life was cut short. For now, she was standing quietly under a tree, minding her own business. With her were Lol-Bey and Muhammad Wang Smith.

Since the zikr, all three had developed a fondness for the desert smells, the green town-trees, and the big lilac bushes that had such deep roots from a century of watering that now they could survive unaided; for the hot, bright sun, and even for the dust storms and tumble weeds. This high desert Earth with its birds and animals, roads and buildings, mountains and cascading streams of snow-melt, sparkling with sunlight in their downward rush, was like nothing they had seen in any galaxy. The architecture, too, was quaint and attractive to them. In the current atmosphere of don't ask/don't tell regarding contact with humans (more about that later), they were the town's most frequent Squidly visitors, though they mostly kept this on the downlow.

One more was with them, an unnamed zi, whose presence and shimmering magenta overtones they politely ignored. This might seem unkind, but it was not. Due to official worries about their effect on the Earthers, all of the zi had been restricted to the ship, and anyone complicit in their disobedience would risk a heavy punishment. Obiwan, Lol-Bey, and Wang

Smith were *indeed* complicit for not reporting the irregularity, but they felt in sympathy with the zi. If one zi was chafing under these unusual restrictions and had managed to slip out, they were fully, though quietly, in support.

These four Squid did not *do* anything when they visited the desert, the mountains, or the town. They just stood silently, sometimes for hours, enjoying the sounds, the colors, the sun, the stars, and most of all, the lovely, lovely smells.

∾

Next night around the Troop's campfire, the conversation continued.

"You heard about them *squid* runnin' around town?" asked Skull with a sly look on his face.

"I heered tell they's good eatin'," said Stetson Black, appearing suddenly. Where the heck had *he* come from? The group knew about the Squid because, though most had left town before their arrival or had never been down there at all, a few had made periodic, secretive trips back to see what was happening.

Stetson Black paused, then said deliberately, "I bet we could *catch* one!"

For a moment everyone was silent, considering the possibilities of an adventure, something new to eat, and a chance to raise some hell.

After a pause, the conversation continued. Wolf and Rap, who should have known better, had gone off to bed in disgust around 1:30. There was something about the atmosphere Stetson Black had created around camp that made any right-thinking person want to get away and wash. The conversations were abysmally stupid and tinged with a racism against the Squid that turned Rap's stomach. Their cadence was all too familiar. Beaner too felt the bad vibrations and slipped away unnoticed.

By 2 a.m., only the worst of the Troop remained, obnoxious yahoos looking for trouble, but estimated by the leadership to be too dumb to cause actual harm. This would have been true but for the presence of Stetson Black.

"Okay, here's what we do," declared Skull with impressive authority. "We sneak up on 'em. I been spying on some of 'em down under that tree, sitting there like a buncha dopes. They's twenty of us and only four of them. We can take 'em easy."

"Each Squid has the strength of fifteen men," said Stetson Black matter-of-factly. "You wouldn't have a chance." This calm statement put a damper on the incipient riot.

"Whudda we do, then?" asked a Trooper. "Does this mean we don't get no f'in barbecue?"

"By no means," said Stetson Black. "It only means we have to trick them. They are strong and quick, and they can swim through time and space, but they know nothing of our customs and will be easy to fool. Here's what we'll do."

⚬

Preisczech sat in his room, pounding his fist gently and rhythmically against the side of his head. He could not forgive himself for his comment that ended the disastrous dinner and he was still unwilling to venture beyond his front steps to see if anyone was talking to him yet. The few people passing by had seemed unusually preoccupied.

How was *he* supposed to know that disgusting thing was some sort of ceremonial gift, sentient and valued beyond measure by the Squids?

He reviewed his reasoning: they were *at* a dinner, they were *eating* dinner, so he had naturally assumed this gift was *for* dinner. Like guests bringing a bottle of wine. And because the idea of eating any portion of the thing appalled him—it would probably have to be consumed raw, possibly even *alive*—he had overcompensated by expressing a forced and grotesque enthusiasm for its consumption.

Not having ventured out, he had no idea of the state of relations between the town and the Squidren post-disaster. He only regretted his mistake and wished he could do something to make it up to everybody. But it did not enter his mind that his ill-considered action had begun a chain reaction that would end by putting innocent beings in deadly danger.

CHAPTER
TWENTY-ONE

Can a creepy man in a black stetson be a shadowy man? Can a shadowy man be a creepy man in a black stetson? Can either or both of them be an old acquaintance of Halycon Sage, a cold, cold writer who wanted to be Sage's nemesis, but whom Sage never noticed at all? Unfortunately, the answer to all these questions is likely to be yes.

What happened next would never have occurred had not the three younger Squid, with only a few centuries' experience, been half in love with the Earth and its beauties. Thus, they were kindly disposed toward the Hoo-mans, ready to learn from them, trust them, and even follow them to an unknown destination.

"How do?" asked the Shadowy Man, stepping from behind a tree.

Obiwan Mohammed had a sinking feeling in her stomachs[19] at the sight and sound of the black-hatted man. But she rejected this first impression, putting it down to her own bias, her natural repugnance toward beings so different in form: dry, shimmerless, and with pitiably few limbs. She had not been at the disastrous dinner, and the power of the *zikr* had overridden similar feelings during her visit to Layla's home. Her contacts with Hoo-mans had been few.

The others were similarly handicapped. Lol-Bey, a sensitive poet, would always strive to empathize with all beings and enter into their experience. A less suspicious creature could hardly be imagined.

Muhammad Wang Smith, a botanist by training and inclination, was contemplating an unusual moss and had become deaf and blind to the outside world. As for the fourth Squid in the group, zi was so pleased to finally be *off that damned ship* that zi would have followed the Devil to a mouse-catching festival.

"How do?" asked the Shadowy Man again, tipping his black stetson. He was backed by Spiffy and a contingent of the Troop. Most of them would have looked rough and dangerous to anyone from Earth, but they looked much like any other humans to the Squids.

"Greetings, Earthling," said Muhammad Wang Smith, who had been prepared for this moment by some old radio broadcasts that TechieSquid had dug up. She had never actually spoken to a Hoo-man before, even at the two shared events.

"So, I hear you liked that Arabic ceremony," said the Shadowy Man, dropping his western affectations. "Would you Squid like to attend a *different* ceremony at our camp? Increase your cultural knowledge? It's only a few miles away."

"Space makes no difference to us, good sir," replied Lol-Bey. "With certain exceptions, we can go anywhere instantaneously."

"What is the ceremony?" Obiwan Mohammed forced down her rising gorge, a mental and emotional unease so strong it had become physical. If she lived through this night, she would never repeat the mistake of ignoring her instinctive alarm system.

"It's called a barbecue," replied the Shadowy Man.

"Humans love it!" put in another Trooper. "In this here country, America, it's our favorite thing to do!"

"Are you sure we would not be intruding?" asked the zi, made cautious by zi's long confinement to the ship.

"*Intruding?*" barked Skull with a laugh. "Hell no, you'll be the guests of honor."

"We will anoint you with a special substance," added Spiffy, "to make you ready for the ceremony. At the culmination, you will lie on a bed of hot coals, something often done by our holy men in pursuit of greater wisdom. It is indeed an honor!"

"May we confer a moment?" asked Obiwan Mohammed.

"Of course," said the black-hatted Man.

The Squidren slithered a few feet away.

"It sounds like an unforgettable cultural experience," said Wang Smith. "An unlooked-for opportunity, not to be missed."

"If it's at all like the zikr . . ." began Lol-Bey hopefully.

"Exactly. It could open new worlds. Think how much we would have to report back to the ship! This could turn the tide, convince the Commander that the Hoo-mans are worth pursuing after all!"

"There's something about that man," murmured Obiwan tentatively, not wanting to give offense or dampen the enthusiasm of the others. That was not the Squidish way.

"I know what you mean, but I think we have to take the chance," replied Lol-Bey.

Muhammad Wang Smith concurred.

The Shadowy Man and his minions turned and walked out toward the mountains, and the Squidiler followed.

A little earlier and not so far away, Preisczech had decided he needed to take action. He couldn't sit on his porch anymore watching former friends pass by, each one looking self-consciously up at the clouds or down at some bug or wildflower to avoid engaging with him. There was no vodka and no computer, nothing to tempt him back into the house. He decided to visit Abdurraheem and see how the glider was progressing. A practical man like himself, and in some sense a fellow scientist, the Iraqi pilot might be congenial to talk to. Their previous interactions had always been positive and subtly satisfying and he was unlikely to be sulking about the dinner party fiasco like everyone else. At least it was something to do.

After a short but invigorating walk, Preisczech found Abdurraheem in his open garage putting the finishing touches on his glider with an air of pleasure and satisfaction.

"Ah, Dr. Preisczech! It is finished. Would you like to come with me to test it?"

Preisczech had almost forgotten his own multiple PhDs, obtained at such a young age. No one seemed to care about such things since the Event.

"Of course, yes, let us test it right now!" The thought of soaring through the air in the powerful, silent thing was exhilarating. It was silvery white, sleek, and beautiful, showing the former pilot and amateur inventor to be a craftsman as meticulous as Preisczech himself.

"We will tow it to *there*," said Abdurraheem, indicating a nearby hill. A sturdy dark blue tow rope was already attached to the metal ring at the front of the plane. "The glider is very light. I will get in, and you will run downhill with the rope until I can take off. You cannot fly today," he added apologetically, "but there is room for two, so sometime soon, if we can enlist some others to help us."

Within a couple of hours, the situation between the Troop and the Squids had escalated into disaster. Near the permanent campfire, a big barbecue pit had been dug. It was filled with red glowing coals, proudly tended by Sparky. This was something new to do, a new relationship with fire!

The Squidiler came, pleased and unresisting, led by the Shadowy Man. The Troop could not believe it. Even cows would not be so stupid! They had procured baseball bats to hit them with and chains to hold them down, to drag them to the fire and keep them there, but none of this was necessary.

"Let us anoint you," said Spiffy, suiting the action to the word. Several Troopers stepped forward, and barbecue sauce was sprinkled ceremoniously over the four unresisting Squid. "It is a great honor for you!"

The anointing completed, the Shadowy Man pointed to the barbecue pit. "Please lie down here. This is the way of our wisemen. This is how it's done."

Lol-Bey took the initiative, lying down upon the burning coals. Squidish pain receptors do not work like those of humans, and the dampness along his skin provided some protection. Still, the Squid was growing increasingly uncomfortable, at an alarming rate, in fact.

"Ouch," said Lol-Bey, hoping he was giving the Earthish distress signal correctly. If these beings realized they were hurting him they would, of course, stop and apologize. Someone would bring cool water to put on his burn.

"Don't worry, you won't feel anything in a little while," said Spiffy cheerfully.

"Ladies," said Stetson Black with a courteous gesture, indicating that the two Squidresses should take their places.

"And zi," he added. *It is evident that he understands our gender identifications and protocols,* thought Muhammad Wang Smith, who had taken a minor in Gender Studies as well as her biology degree.

Something is very wrong here, thought Obiwan Mohammed.

The three remaining Squidren complied, unsure yet willing.

"Ouch!" said Lol-Bey again, more loudly. These Hoomans were obviously not getting the message. His outer coating of slime had been breached by the heat, and he was beginning to smoke. "Ouch, ouch!!!"

"Please, sir, we are sentient beings!" cried Obiwan Mohammed, convinced, like all of them, that some monstrous mistake was happening. The intensity of her thought was so strong that the effect was almost of spoken, shouted words.

Skull did not know what *sentient* meant, but he got the idea.

"I don't cotton to your fancy alien words," said Skull, unconsciously slipping into an old-western mode of speech, "but I guess I get your drift. You're tryna tell me you're like *me*. But, see, I don't think you *are* like me, because you got too many legs and you're a funny color blue."

He was enjoying all the eyes upon him, being the center of attention. He knew how to hold an audience, that was for sure.

"Tell you the truth," he continued, shifting into a stage-whisper, "I don't even think *Beaner and Big D here* are like me, 'cause they got funny colors *too*, walkin' around like they just naturally need a bath."

If No-Name Stupid, Basel Vasselschnauzer, or Emma had been there, they would have appreciated the irony, as Skull was not known for bathing.

He addressed Lol-Bey directly. "So, see, I don't care if you *cry*, or if you *scream*, or if some of these here ugly aliens are supposed to be *ladies* because my friends and me's wantin' some barbecue and, well, here you are." Skull stood back with a self-satisfied smirk. He did not take in the remarkably blank expressions on the faces of Beaner and Big D. And he had another problem too, though he did not know it. Someone was coming. Several someones.

"In fact," Skull was on a roll now, "if you cry, it might even make you *taste better*. A little *saltwater*, you know?" He looked around, smirking, at his appreciative audience.

Muhammad Wang Smith, who had come partially out of her scholar's trance, was still hoping to enlighten these seemingly obtuse creatures.

"Squid do not cry salt tears," she said faintly.

Stetson Black, the Shadowy Man, walked over to Lol-Bey and looked directly, deliberately into his eyes. Lol-Bey looked back. He did not see the misunderstanding and stupidity that, for him, would have made sense of this insane situation. He saw complacency, satisfaction, and cruelty. As eyes looked into eyes, realization dawned.

"Yes," said the Shadowy Man. "You're right, it's not a mistake. We're going to kill all four of you. Painfully. On purpose. And then we're going to eat you. And you'll taste delicious!"

The Squid lay blank and silent.

"Don't you get it?" cried Skull. "WE'RE GOING TO EAT YOU!"

"EAT YOU!" chorused all the Troopers.

Squidren do not faint or pass out. But apparently—this was uncharted territory—when stress becomes too great and access to the healing Squidpool is denied, they go into a kind of shock: no feelings, no actions, no thoughts. So the captured Squidiler suddenly ceased the continuous, automatic transmission of thoughts, feelings, and locations by which the Squidren keep track of each other. This turned out to be a serious problem.

CHAPTER
TWENTY-TWO

emember where we left Preisczech and Abdurraheem? Let us refresh your memory. "You cannot fly today," Abdurraheem added apologetically, "but there is room for two, so sometime soon, if we can enlist some others to help us."

There was a sudden disturbance, and they were not alone. From a darkish corner of the garage—and why were odd and wonderful things always emerging from dark corners in this strange, new world?—came an assembly of Squidresses. The clear leader was a magnificent being, eight feet tall, deep, shimmering, sparkling blue shading to purple. Beside her was a small, nondescript Squidlet, barely five feet tall, of flat, unrelieved satin black and bearing with her a kind of listening silence. *Her handmaiden*, thought Preisczech wildly.

There slowly appeared several more, coming into focus like beings not quite corporeal: three or five or seven slightly indistinct forms, shorter than the leader but still impressive, ranked behind her and to the sides. They formed a narrow triangle, a phalanx of powerful beings, the Leader at its head. They reminded Abdurraheem of a Chinese picture he had seen once, a high princess flanked by her ladies. These ladies were both beautiful attendants and powerful guards, a suggestion of yellow and pink silk robes about them, fans in their supple hands. All of that was here too.

"We are so sorry to disturb you," declared the Lady, "but we must commandeer your glider. There is desperate need. You sir, must fly it, and you (to Preisczech) can ride along."

"But I need to be outside to pull the tow rope," objected Preisczech.

"We can take care of that," replied the Squidress with some authority.

"What exactly is the problem?" inquired the pilot courteously. He was cautiously friendly but had not yet committed himself.

The tall, beautiful Squid gave a sigh.

"Some yahoos, I believe you call them?" Abduraheem and Preisczech looked at each other, clueless.

"Some yahoos," repeated the Lady more firmly, "have taken some of our children. Three innocent Squidlets of two or three hundred years, along with a fully mature zi who should have known better. They have been lured away, for a purpose more hideous than we have encountered in all our cross-dimensional travels."

This was impressive and potentially upsetting. Preisczech was glad he was with Abdurraheem and not with Halycon Sage, who would probably have burst into tears. Well, no, he was not *that* bad, but he would have gone into some extended rumination or diatribe about good and evil, which would not have helped at all.

"They have committed a terrible crime and intend to commit another," continued the Lady.

Something was bothering Preisczech.

"Forgive me, I have it from grapevine . . ." He stopped doubtfully. What he was saying sounded ridiculous, yet he was sure it was correct. "From *grapevine*, I say, that you Squid have strength of many humans and can transport your bodies easily anywhere. Why cannot these Squid children escape by themselves? Or, if not, why cannot you save them? Why you need glider to rescue them?"

"Because they've stopped transmitting. We don't know where they are. The last thing we received from their minds was the impression of a rough camp in the mountains and something called 'the Troop.' But we have no idea where it is! There are mountains all around us, and time is limited."

"What crime have the humans committed?" Abduraheem asked carefully.

"*Squidnapping*," replied the Lady with the utmost seriousness. "We need you to help us rescue them!"

Abdurraheem almost imagined tears in her eyes, though to his knowledge, the Squid did not cry.

"And what further crime do they contemplate?" he asked her.

"*Barbecue*."

"Let's go," said both men together. If there were people anywhere on Earth or in the Alternate Universe who would have refused such a call, Alexander Lazlo Preisczech and Muhammad Abduraheem Hussein were not among them.

They were in for one more surprise. As the strange party walked the glider toward the hill, Emma, waitress and sometime manager of the ~~Dirty Dog~~ Canis Fidelis Grill and Juice Bar, suddenly stepped out from behind the assembly of Squidresses. Smiling, she extended her hands, offering the two surprised humans a plate of warm, fragrant chocolate chip cookies.

Finding the Troop's camp was not easy; it took a while. No one in the glider had been there, and nobody knew much beyond, "It's about a quarter way up one of the mountains."

Perhaps even more important, no ordinary pilot could have caught the updrafts and downwinds so expertly, guiding the plane exactly where they needed to go.

Suddenly, "*There!*" shouted Abdurraheem, pointing. A small fire was burning in a nearby valley. He looked around for a landing place and, with consummate skill, made preparations to bring the glider down. Once again, the pilot's impressive competence and professionalism were proving invaluable. His eagle eye, as well. He had seen the fire before anyone else, even the Squidren.

It was certainly good that Immigration decided to let him back in after all! Preisczech had heard the story, and it had been a near thing. If the country's door had been slammed in the Iraqi's face, where would they all be now?

Help came from three directions. First, Beaner and Big D simultaneously decided that Skull was an intolerable, hateful, idiotic *Norte Americano* honkey pipsqueak (or something to that effect) and that they would foil his plans to barbecue the prisoners. The whole idea was sick anyway, reminding them forcibly of things that had been done to their ancestors.

Big D *did* know what sentient meant, while Beaner, who had a distinct copper cast to his skin, kept thinking about the Conquistadors. Looking around, they saw that Rap had arrived and they caught his eye.

"No!" said Rap stepping forward. "Just no. Sparky?"

Big D, always cautious, always the guardian, had brought two heavy buckets of water in case of accidents. Deliberately, he grappled one up off the ground and passed it to Sparky. Sparky was proud. His moment had come. He could help his mentor and serve Fire in a new way, by restraining it from committing harm. There had been some breakthrough in his dim consciousness, and he suddenly realized that the Squid had *feelings*. He threw the water directly over Lol-Bey, raising a great cloud of steam. Big D nodded to him approvingly and threw the second bucketful.

Next, Beaner stepped over to Obiwan Mohammed, Big D to Muhammad Wang Smith, and Rap to the unidentified zi, as yet unsmoking, but certainly in danger. Their courteous inquiries were ignored by the unresponsive Squids. Rap and Big D exchanged a bemused glance across the fallen bodies, which seemed to be losing some of their sparkle and color.

"We could try chaffing their wrists," said Big D.

Wow. This dude was *something*. Like almost everyone in the post-Event world, he had hidden depths. *Been watching them Victorian dramas again,* thought Rap. *Or, not watching them, but* remembering *them anyway.*

He looked across the aliens at his colleague.

"*What* wrists?" he asked rhetorically.

Help came from three directions, and the second direction was the sky. Suddenly, a mind-stilling coolness, damp and fresh, transformed the landscape and the sweet rain began to fall. The last remains of the barbecue fire were reduced to a gentle hiss, harmless and rebuked.

From the third direction came the glider, graceful as a gull, a dream of silver-white. Without a sound, it landed, and strange visitors stepped from its open door.

The glider only held two, Abdurraheem and Preisczech, but this had not been a problem. The Squidresses had somehow ridden along, sitting on the roof, or on the wings, or clinging gently to the belly of the plane. Since they did not *weigh* anything—as Lol-

Bey had suspected for a long time, the Squid had no actual mass—they had not pulled the plane off course.

Since only two humans could be accommodated, Emma had stayed behind at Abdurraheem and Layla's house, with MysterySquid to keep her company. When Layla came home she made tea to go with the rest of the cookies. MysterySquid came out of her shell far enough to inhale the fragrances with obvious enjoyment.

But we digress: Back to the camp.

"Ahem," said the Leader, trying out a word she had seen in human writings gleaned from TechieSquid. She did not know that this was a throat-clearing noise, having no idea of a throat, much less what clearing it might entail.

Skull got the point at once. They were *busted*. They were *good* and busted, they were *dead*. Though she was eight feet tall, tentacled and blue, the Leader reminded him of an English teacher he'd once had. Hot flashes of humiliating memory poured over him, obscuring even the danger. He looked around for the Shadowy Man, but he was nowhere to be seen. *Real nice,* thought Skull. *Get me into this mess and then leave me holding the bag.*

"We was gonna club 'em first," Skull babbled hurriedly, looking for some defense. "We wasn't gonna cook 'em *alive*. We didn't know they was *people*."

"Yes, they did," said Beaner, looking at the Empress. (Oh, er, we mean . . . the Leader.)

"They surely did, ma'am," confirmed Big D, looking at her as well. This large, slow-moving man, whose face betrayed so little, had figured out for himself that the purple-blue Squidren were female and that the big one was the leader. Perhaps if the new world survived, there would be a place for him beyond the mere babysitting of poor Sparky.

There was a stirring on the ground, and the prisoners returned to consciousness. Suddenly, showing their strange adaptability that sometimes followed alien contact, the Squid began to cry. Tears streamed down their green-blue, purpley-blue, and magenta-blue faces. It was not a reaction of relief after the fear of a painful death, nor was it sorrow for the horror they had been through, or even compassion for their captors, so sunk in ignorance and darkness. The tears were precipitated by the presence of the Lady, the Leader, and by the smell of falling rain on sagebrush, the honest-to-God sweetest smell in all the worlds.

PART FOUR

THE BUILD-UP

WHEREIN the Yellow Thread is unveiled and illumined. For without the orangey-yellow cat, what follows could never have happened.

CHAPTER
TWENTY-THREE

Interlude: Didn't this book start with foreshadowing about time travel?

Halycon Sage's first hint had that he might be dealing with time travelers was this: He found that a twentieth century author had stolen an idea that had occurred to him only yesterday. The idea was that his imaginary author, 'Karima Vargas Bushnell,' might, in an alternate universe, be writing a book about *him*—had, in fact, written his autobiography, *The Way Beyond*, the identical book but presented as fiction.

Yet the next day, *the very next day after he had this thought*, he discovered the same idea in an absurdity called *Novel* by one Rupert Griffin[20]. There was a suggestion that the protagonist, a writer, might have made up Griffin as one of his characters. Surely this strange thought could not have occurred to two separate individuals with no link of cause and effect between them! And Sage certainly hadn't gotten the idea from Griffin. He had never heard of Griffin or *Novel* until he found it one morning behind the bar at the Dirty Dog. He had certainly not thumbed or flipped through it and unconsciously absorbed the idea. In the matter of reading, he was a traditionalist who did not cheat, but always proceeded respectfully from page one to page two and so forth.

The fact that a mere day separated Sage's flash of inspiration from his discovery, in Griffin, of something as like it as dammit, was only susceptible to one explanation. Griffin had stolen his idea. And since *Novel* was written long before Sage *had* the idea, the only possible conclusion was that Griffin was a low down, thieving time traveler.

While Sage was thinking these things, the committees were in session over at the Dirty Dog. All was not well. Food had fractured again, this time splitting into the vegan/vegetarian contingent and, briefly, the bow hunters and trappers. The ovo-lacto vegetarians were detested by everybody, seen as self-deluding sybarites by the vegans and pathetic eco-wimps by the carnivores.

Even more detested were the trappers, whom everyone else denounced for their cruelty. They were made to go and sit at a table by themselves.

✍

It was odd what had happened about the Cuttlefish. After the horrible debacle at the dinner party, the more thoughtful members of the community expected a complete rift with the Squids. The alien contingent had turned as one and flowed out of the room, not even politely pretending to use the door but simply melting through the front wall. Such was their degree of outrage.

The humans, of course, fell to bickering and blaming each other: for acting rashly and speaking stupidly; for failing to recognize sincere, though misguided, good intentions; for not attending meetings where vital information had been shared; and for not sharing the information that would have prevented disaster. Sage stayed out of this mess. He was Indian enough not to make things worse when all he needed to do was be silent.

Layla had run out of the room after Nuri. One Squid apparently followed her through the bedroom wall, but in all the chaos, only Sophie had observed this and she forgot about it till later. Everyone else had finally calmed down and begun discussing the matter seriously, agreeing that the humans had offered the Squidiler some deadly insult and that it would be very difficult to put relations back on a positive footing.

It was quickly discovered that there were two schools of thought on how to proceed. (Imaginary author Karima Vargas Bushnell could have explained the dynamics, possessing, as she did, an imaginary master's degree in Intercultural Relations.) Some people thought,

"Least said, soonest mended." Sweep the controversy under the rug, pretend it never happened, and greet the Squid, on the next meeting, with the same casual or ceremonial friendliness as always.

The second group thought this was ridiculous. Everyone knows that a boil must not be left to fester but must be lanced! A problem swept under the rug merely grows bigger, accumulating dust and mold and … well, never mind.

Their imagery grew more disgusting as their vehemence increased. It soon became obvious that neither side could see the other's point of view and that neither would budge. It was agreed that each individual would follow their own inclinations when next encountering a Squid. Then it could be seen which method worked best.

Just as this conclusion was reached, Layla re-entered the room and added that she would say a prayer for all concerned. This was received with a spectrum of facial expressions and brief phrases ranging from honest gratitude to kindly contempt, and everybody went home.

As it turned out, while the Squidiler kept a lower profile after the dinner, some of them were still quietly visiting the town. Thus, Layla was able to issue her invitation and request that it be passed on. Given the tension between the two species, the Squid identified as Muslims were just as pleased that the zikr meeting was clandestine.

What was forgotten in this welter of guesswork, politics, and outraged feelings demonstrated the human proclivity for getting lost in the details and missing the vital point. Nobody thought to ask what had happened to the Cuttlefish.

Unvirtual Time Travel
"Real Experiences for Real People"

The sign on the door looked great. It was made of real wood, with real paint on it, which showed what remarkable things could be done with access to the past. Though molecular color change was supposed to be flawless, reproducing any previous technique or artistry, this just looked different. Its presence on the door was advertising genius since it proclaimed irrefutably that the agency could do what it claimed: move beyond ho-hum virtual time travel with screens and images to transporting actual objects, and maybe even the physical bodies of its customers, to their desired elsewhens.

No longer was the past a mere peep show, a dull mediated experience to be seen from a distance. Unvirtual Time Travel . . . *takes . . . you . . . there!*

<u>Interview</u>

Q. So, Mr. Griffin, how long has your company been in business?

A. Agency, please.

Q. Your agency, then. How long?

A. (Chuckling) Well, that's sort of hard to say. You could say we've been in business since 5000 B.C.E. since that's the farthest back we've taken anybody.

Q. That's evasive. You're playing games with time.

A. My dear sir, that is what we *do*. We play games with time, for the enjoyment and edification of the travelling public.

Q. Okay, when did a bunch of *froods*[21] sit down and cook up this idea?

A. Maybe the 80s, but let's move on. The important thing is not *when*, but *what*. No one else in the galaxy has this technology. We're absolutely cutting edge!
Voice Off-Camera: Excuse me, sir, it's time for your appointment with the Northern Barbarians.

A. Thank you, Miss O'Connell. I'm sorry ladies and gentlemen, duty calls.

In the Alternate Universe, the Cat Fatty Lumpkin belonged to the imaginary author, Karima Vargas Bushnell, and within her family, a certain kind of romantic hero/villain from book and film was known as "a Fatty Lumpkin." *Par example*, George Wickham of *Pride and Prejudice*[22].

The term implied, among other things, a handsome and dashing scoundrel with limitless self-confidence. While the cat himself was endlessly loving and loyal to his human and feline friends, he was aware of the term and chose to take it as a compliment to his beauty and intelligence rather than as a slur on his morals. And he liked stories about these characters supposedly like himself.

Here in the real world of Dry Creek Gulch, Fatty was currently in the room behind the bar at the Dirty Dog, trying to read *The Prisoner of Zenda*, which included a ginger-haired character much to his liking. Reading was a vexatious task, however, straining not his intellect, but his physical form. Why had Creator not given him thumbs? How was he supposed to turn the pages?

Sliding a paw along the slippery sheet, separating one wafer-thin piece from another, coaxing the just-read piece back to reveal the forthcoming one—this was a far more delicate and frustrating process than his previous exploits of opening kitchen cabinets and canisters of cat food or swinging doors that baffled the other cats. And two differently designed refrigerators. It was even harder than ricocheting a large rolling chair back to a food-bearing kitchen table after Mother had pushed it away. And that was one trick the humans were never able to explain.

CHAPTER
TWENTY-FOUR

*The Funny Thing that Happened
to Halycon Sage*

Halycon Sage had pretty much forgotten his secret food stash. Now when he visited the cave, he stood or sat all day in front of the wall, waiting patiently to see if any new writing or pictures showed up. One day he was rewarded, but not exactly in the way he'd been expecting. Instead of letters or video developing, a small hole appeared in the surface of the wall.

While he was looking at the hole, wondering what would happen next, a second hole appeared. They were irregularly shaped and located on different parts of the wall. He could see a bit of light coming through them, but nothing on the other side.

Then came a booming, authoritative voice. "Halycon Sage."

He was silent.

"Halycon Sage," it said again, more emphatically this time. It sounded like somebody's idea of God from a bad old movie.

He resisted the temptation to say, "That's my name, don't wear it out." He waited patiently, and then, when the interval seemed long enough to demonstrate good manners, responded in the affirmative. The voice changed abruptly, becoming lighter and more modern-sounding, yet still serious and portentous.

"Halycon Sage, are you very, very brave? Are you willing to accept a great responsibility?"

"Well, I dunno. Sometimes I'm brave. Can you tell me more about the parameters? Would I get to have Stupid with me? I mean it kind of depends on whether—"

There was an abrupt popping noise and the two holes in the wall disappeared. Still, Sage felt that somehow his very conditional and tentative acceptance of some unknown task had been received. *I'm in it now,* thought Halycon Sage.

CHAPTER
TWENTY-FIVE

alycon Sage was writing day and night in a one-pointed fury of concentration. Doubly obsessed with his alternate universe and the periodic appearance of the softly glowing, flame-shaped letters on the cave wall—not to mention Ratbone's strange video and the two holes which now came and went at random moments—he had taken his writing supplies, sleeping bag, a can opener and some cans of beans and moved into the cave.

Ruby was convinced that she had pushed him too far, driving him away through her constant nagging about meetings and community activities and that she needed to leave him alone for a while. She was calm about this. As one of the de facto leaders of the community, she had plenty to do without babysitting an eccentric writer who seemed to be off his feed. He would come back when he was ready.

Also, nobody knew exactly where he was. Sage was a large man with long legs; in absent-mindedly walking further than he had intended that first day, he had entered remote regions of the cave, putting not just yards, but miles behind him. It was also possible that the cave itself had expanded since his arrival or had put up some kind of protective barrier to shield him from the curious. His reality had always been fluid, and never more so than now, when so many strange variables had been introduced into his existence. Now he had become fixated on his latest book to the point where everything else seemed unreal.

He had written the Alternate Universe into a horrid mess and had no idea how to get it out again. The book had become heavy with tragedy and desperation. All humor, spirituality, and fine shades of meaning were gone. A sodden wodge of paper towels indeed! The nasty dictator of the United States, introduced on a whim as a minor character, had pretty much taken over the story. He and his minions were everywhere, taking everything apart as effectively as the Nanobots, but with far less noble purpose.

Preisczech, after all, had been trying to save the world, convinced that nuclear catastrophe, environmental disaster, and wholesale destruction through war profiteering and weapons sales were the worst looming dangers and could only be averted by neutralizing their foundational technologies.

Perhaps none of this mattered. As far as Sage knew, the Alternate Universe was purely imaginary, a creation of his own that, in the story, had split off from reality at the moment the Nanobots were invented. It was also quite possible that no one would ever find time to read the book when it was finished.

Originally a sort of accidental writer, Sage had come to take pride in his work and he wanted it to be good. He did not *like* writing about the horrid dictator and all the alienation. This depressing, soggy mess could lose him the two readers he actually *had*, and he was determined to write something better. Something more lively and interesting and less like a bad B movie about the future.

He looked down, hearing a gentle thrumming noise. There was that striped cat again, making himself comfortable on the Navajo blanket Sage had let fall sloppily at his feet. He usually preferred a blanket to a coat, though this had occasioned derision in some quarters. You could do a lot more with a blanket.

The cat rolled sideways, exposing a white stomach, stippled with apricot-colored patterns. This stomach was clearly desirous of attention. Halycon Sage absently stirred the cat with his bare foot, increasing the volume of the purring. This cat might be good company if he'd stick around a little longer, but he always vanished after a few minutes. Where he went was a mystery.

Back on the ship, the Squid were having a discussion. It was back to business as usual: trying to find a different Earth species to partner with, guiding Halycon Sage, attempting to corral the Nanobots, and doing whatever else needed doing to clean up the appalling mess the Earthers had created.

No matter what epiphanies and traumas they had experienced, everyone had to look and act normal, even the recently rescued targets of the Late Great Attempted Barbecue, who had not only been bowled over by the threat of a hideous death but by the sight of their rescuer. Meeting her was the honor of a lifetime, not to be dreamed of except for a very few. But they were sworn to secrecy. As far as they knew, no one on the ship knew of their adventure.

There had been some disagreement after the disastrous dinner as to whether further contact with the Hoo-mans was advisable. Squid culture was interesting in that it could be either hierarchical or egalitarian depending on the circumstances. When there was a major disagreement among persons of roughly equal authority, there was a tendency to let each side try its own solution and base final decisions on the results.

Thus, some Squid had been avoiding the Earth people altogether, while others, like the barbecue targets, had kept interacting with them on the down low. As already reported, the semi-secret nature of Layla's zikr had suited them well, enabling them to be discrete in their continued interactions. But now enough time had passed to observe the species more closely. In order to move forward, the achieving of consensus or the giving of an order was necessary.

COMMANDER JOHN KENNEDY: To sum up, the Hoo-mans (and the Hoo-womans and Hoo-zi as well), in spite of earlier indications, have proven conclusively that they cannot be the dominant species on this planet and are probably not even sentient as we understand the term. We have approached the wrong species!

(The Commander hoped devoutly that his persuasion would succeed so he could avoid issuing an unexplained order on the one hand, or describing the attempted barbecue on the other. He had read about it in the two different sources provided by TechieSquid, but it had been kept Top Secret from all the others. While he favored disengaging with the Hoo-mans, he did not want the officers to feel compelled to destroy them.)

(The calm focus exhibited by some of the younger Squidiler would have amazed Kennedy had he known, which he did not, that they themselves had been the subjects of the horrifying incident.)

JOHN CHANG: I concur. We must correct the error at once. According to our preliminary survey, there are at least two species of more likely beings, and we are fortunate to have one of each within our circle of acquaintance. I suggest we approach them both to find out which is dominant.

FOUR: (Ignoring Chang, whom she found to be a pill.) Might we hear your reasons, Commander? This seems hasty, to say the least, and wasteful after all the work we have put in.

KENNEDY: Well, the dinner party seems definitive. Surely no civilization worthy of the name would have reacted in such a way to the Gift of the Cuttlefish. That alone demonstrates their barbarity.

FOUR: But what about the zikr? A feast of sound, light, and movement that replenished us for weeks. And it was not accidental. It was done very consciously.

(Though she had not been on the guest list, Four had conscientiously read the summaries from the Mohammeds and Lol-Bey and was intrigued.)

KENNEDY: There are always outliers.

CHANG: I still haven't heard anything conclusive. What is your clinching argument?

(Chang must have been briefed before the meeting by the Commander, who wanted this question asked. Four knew this to be so because Chang would never have challenged the Commander in this way if it hadn't been set up beforehand, especially since he had just artlessly blurted out that he agreed with him. *Suck-up*, she thought.)

KENNEDY: They don't create any literature! Or oral culture either. Only three Hoo-mans out of the whole village have created any sagas whatsoever! This *proves* that they are not sapient beings!

FOUR: (Defensively): Layla writes!

KENNEDY: Recipes!

SEVERAL SQUID (Chiming in): But what about Halycon Sage? A world-famous author before the Event! The sole creator of the whole Post-Modernist Minimalist Neo-Symbolist Pseudo-Realist School of Literature!

KENNEDY: And most of what he writes is unmitigated drivel! Why else have we exiled it to Appendix B?

There could be no arguing with this. The Squidiler paused for a few days to contemplate the arc of their discussion.

OBIWAN MOHAMMED: But what about these other species? Do *they* write?

MUHAMMAD WANG SMITH: They *do* compose literature and appear capable of broadcasting it mentally. At least we have picked it up. (FOUR nods.)

TECHIESQUID: The representatives of both species we have encountered write poetry. One hundred percent of the sample, so perhaps they *all* do.

KENNEDY: Alright, we'll approach them. Who knows the Stripe-ed One?

LOL-BEY: I have been observing him carefully and believe we may have built a rapport. I attended to a deposit he left behind after the zikr; surely, he must be grateful.

KENNEDY: Very well then. And you might read him some of your *own* poetry. What about the One With Hooves?

FOUR: I have not spoken with him, but I have given him, on two occasions, an apple and a lump of sugar. He seemed pleased.

KENNEDY: Very well. The mass is ended. Go in peace.

Kennedy had picked up this phrase from one of TechieSquid's intercepted television broadcasts and considered it an elegant close to any gathering. Besides, it had something to do with his namesake's reference group, so was doubly appropriate.

The Squidiler were pleased and most shifted their focus from the Hoo-mans to cats and horses, finding mounting evidence that these were indeed the dominant species. Unfortunately for their plans, Fatty Lumpkin and No-Name Stupid were not exactly typical.

In the welter of details to be attended to, there was another thing that was missed. Nobody had really considered how it was that TechieSquid was receiving and sharing Earthean broadcasts since the requisite technology was dead and they were not far enough away to be picking up sounds from the past. This turned out to be important.

John Chang wished that just once he could say or do something in front of Four without sounding like a blithering idiot, an aggressive jerk, or a pompous blowhard. He was senior, universally respected, and generally had an easy grace that made him liked by all. But this deployment was different.

He was *interested* in Four, that was the problem. He had not felt like this in centuries, and it was making his job difficult to do. She was such a stubborn, irritating, yet completely intriguing Squidress! Alone among the Squidiler, she refused to reveal her Earth name. She had apparently refrained from the generally approved choices of John, Muhammad, Chang, Wang, and Smith or variations thereof. She had picked her own very individualized name, maintaining that it was unnecessary to share it with anyone since she was working alone and part of her work was an undercover assignment. Only MysterySquid was more persistently secretive. If Chang had known that her Earth name was Mata Hari Alsatia Epinephrine Venetia McTaggart, he would have been even more intrigued.

CHAPTER
TWENTY-SIX

Meanwhile, Halycon Sage had worn himself out with writing and was having a daydream. It held no complications. No strange cave, no Alternate Universe, no Squid. Just honest townspeople developing their skills, working harmoniously to save the world.

In Sage's daydream, he was giving an interview. This was something the mysterious writer had often done in his previous life, either over the radio through a voice distorter or on television from within his impenetrable disguise.

Since there was no more TV or radio, he set his daydream at the public library, that resurgent locus of literature and culture, which was growing ever more popular as procedures for everything developed and people had a little time on their hands.

But somehow his imagining went wrong. The subject was his new novel, *Stranger,* and he was being interviewed by a tidy woman before a small audience—

without benefit of a microphone since such no longer existed.

"So, Mr. Sage, is your new novel about an exciting and change-producing stranger, a mysterious and frightening stranger, an intriguing and romantic stranger?" asked the interviewer.

"No," said Halycon Sage.

Reader, have you forgotten the Nanobots? While this is understandable and forgivable, please know that the Nanobots have not forgotten *themselves*. In fact, it might be stated that the Nanobots have remembered themselves for the first time. As you shall see.

—Sophie McGregor et al., with permission of the editors.

Introducing the Red (and Silver) Thread: What Red Button?

Nano Prime One stared at the apparition before him. Until this moment, the Nanobots had gone about their business systematically and without emotion, dismantling nuclear weapons, handguns, gas-powered lawn mowers, and fancy electric ice cream machines—anything not exempted by their eccentric inventor, Alexander Preisczech—with equal detachment. They followed their assigned mission: the only practical method, Preisczech and Sage had finally concluded, of averting global suicide. The Nanobots were *machines*, and thus did not think, wonder, deviate, or speculate. And they were all alike, millions upon millions of them. Until this one fateful day.

Nano Prime One stared at the apparition before him. To make a creation come alive as an independent entity, a shock is required. A shock, physical, psychological, emotional, or metaphysical. Something to wake the entity up, to shake it out of its trance of thingness. Those who know speculate that the trigger was the coincidental involvement of Red and Silver. For the Nanobots, though microscopic, are Red and Silver, as anyone who has read the Chronicle can testify. Long before the image below was contemplated, the Nanobots were Red and Silver.

Regard the image. Consider its implications. Consider its possible effect upon an unawakened creature whose rudimentary sense of selfhood contains only the most limited data: the unexamined, half-unconscious knowledge that, "I am a Nanobot. We Nanobots are Red and Silver. We take things apart, Preisczech is our master, and we are Red and Silver." For the button is *entirely silver!* The only red is *on the label*!

The world's enlightened teachers know, as do the adepts and dabblers who unwisely attempt to bring the inanimate to life, that to awaken a creation as an independent entity capable of free will, a shock is required. Even Dr. Frankenstein knew this. Cast in a positive light, this shock is called Satori, Awakening, Enlightenment.

Knowing all this, regard the image below, and consider its possible effect on an innocent, nameless Nanobot, one of millions upon millions, merely minding its mindless business and taking apart all the machines in the world. [If your planet is in grayscale, click here (https://karimavargasbushnell.com/what-red-button/) to see the colors.[23]]

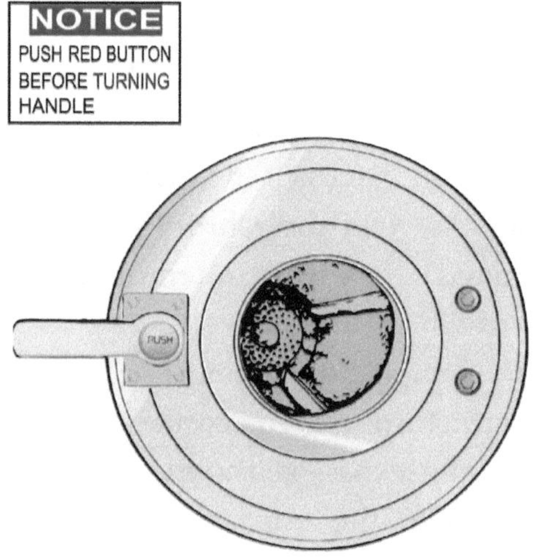

CHAPTER
TWENTY-SEVEN

How the Blue and Green Threads Converged and How the (First) End of the World Came About: What the Squid Did

At some point in the history of Earth, most people forgot they were supposed to be caretakers, keeping all things in balance, maintaining the Sacred Hoop. They stopped caring. And while the endlessly giving planet, that cornucopia of air, water, minerals, nutrients, plants, and animals, was able to sustain this abuse for a time, eventually it was played out.

Thus, the Green Thread Was Dying.

The Squidren, swimming through time and space in the vicinity of Earth, looked down upon it in shock. Searching every mind, they at last found the Mind Meld between Sage and Preisczech, the small fulcrum that could lift the world. And they used this tool with all their skill to save the planet.

They had not realized that an intervention so massive would create a fork in the road, a splitting of the EarthWorld into one reality where the Great Event had occurred and another where it had not. They had half hoped to conceal this mistake from their superiors so many light years away, but this turned out to be impossible.

The EarthWorld, perhaps not so significant in itself, had dragged most of the known universe with it when it split. There were now two of everything, at least in most of the galaxies accessible to the appalled Squid team. Only the senior members of the expedition were aware of the whole situation, the younger ones being considered unable to absorb the news. The chances were three to one that, upon finding that their intervention had pretty much ripped everything apart, these young ones would dive into the anxiety-dissolving Squidpool and never come out.

Just to put the icing on the cake, the Nanobots had inexplicably awakened as sentient beings, and their subsequent development had taken an utterly unanticipated direction. From Nano Prime One, the condition had spread; thousands of woke Nanobots were swarming everywhere. Following their original directive, they were still trying save to the world, but now this activity was guided by their own diagnosis of the problem and its proper solution, ideas severely limited by their lack of understanding and experience of almost everything. The universe was split, the Squidish officers were in big trouble back home, the self-directed Nanobots were unleashed, and in the Alternate Universe, Earth was still dying. Everything was going wrong.

Still holed up in his cave, Sage veered wildly between obsessively writing his alternate reality novel, now over 400 pages and getting worse every day, and doing almost anything that would distract him from it. Also, he was missing Ruby terribly and trying not to think about her. There was something wrong with time here, and he had no idea how long he had been away. More strangely, his supply of baloney did not seem to be diminishing. Ruby was an independent and resourceful woman, strong and beautiful into the bargain. Would she even *want* him back?

On one of these off-days, he decided to write to Rupert Griffin, presumed time traveler/thief and the author of *Novel*. He had no address for the man, and in fact had no idea whether he was alive or dead, but his idea was to tuck the letter into one of the holes in the wall, let it vanish into wherever such things went, and hope for the best.

Since he had no idea whether this was even possible, he thought the experiment was worth a try, and since the whole project was merely a way of wasting time, he was not greatly invested in its success. It beat counting the tiny stalactites.

Dear Professor Griffin,

Your book Novel is darned near perfect and almost makes me ashamed to call myself a writer, though I was initially shocked and concerned that you had stolen my idea of a character writing an author while the author was writing them. Being pretty sure that two people could not have come up with this unique idea completely at random, independently—how likely is that?—I jumped to the unwarranted conclusion that you were an unprincipled time traveler who had been spying on me and had stolen my idea. Seeing that you, like myself, are concerned with time, freedom, and light, this did not seem all that unlikely. Please excuse this hasty and libelous conclusion! I know better now.

Perhaps if you are still alive and have some means of transportation—and if the Perimeter barrier around our town, which is probably being imposed by alien Squid, can be penetrated for the purpose of delivering this letter, receiving your response, and enabling us to rendezvous— we could have a cup of coffee sometime and discuss our mutual interests.

But I digress. The real reason I'm writing to you is about the dog. You know, the black dog at the beginning of Novel? Sir, I beg you to reconsider. You must spare the dog! It is not right, what happens. I know you can fix this

*because you are not averse to playing with time
and space. It would be easy!*
   Yours truly,
   Halycon Sage.

As it happened, Professor Griffin *did* see the letter. And because he had not yet discovered the massive anomaly that would send him in frantic search of Halycon Sage or the Squidren, the author chuckled to himself. For indeed, he was in no wise averse to playing with time and space.

CHAPTER
TWENTY-EIGHT

No-Name Stupid was bored. Though he considered himself a horse of many resources, they had almost run out. He did his fair share of hauling and taxiing, but there were other creatures to help with this now, including the Zombie's brown mule, and he still had a lot of time on his hands (or hooves).

His closest human friends, so dependable before the Event, had become increasingly unreliable. Ruby was always busy with committee work, organizing, and hands-on physical labor. Halycon Sage, his erstwhile owner—though both of them found this concept offensive—was nowhere to be found.

Stupid had achieved all the things he'd wished for while confined in various motel rooms waiting for Halycon Sage to get it together, find himself, save the world or whatever other muddle-brained human enterprise he was engaged in. Stupid had run through long, sweet grass, and eaten it too. He had felt the wind in his mane. He had clopped down dirt roads exploring and enjoying the dusty sun-smell of the west. He had even found himself a nice female horse, and come to an agreement with her, an intention documented in the previous Chronicle.

Editor's Note: If anyone is wondering how Sage managed to keep a stallion in a motel room—doing this with a gelding seems improbable enough—well, we know that Halycon Sage is a man of mystery with many talents, Stupid is a horse quite beyond the ordinary run, and you've already accepted the possibility of time travel, alternate universes, and interdimensional telepathic Squid, have you not? Well then.

Stupid had also enjoyed apples and sugar, provided both by human friends and by these odd *blue ones* who had recently appeared, the big slithery ones who talked to him with their minds instead of their mouths. To Stupid, it was pretty much six of one and half a dozen of the other between the blue ones and the humans. He had a deep affection for Sage, Ruby, and a few others, but trying to get most humans to understand the simplest thing was like talking to mud.

As it turns out, the stallion-in-motel problem had been solved, not through some mysterious power of Halycon Sage nor by any literary trick or willful blindness to writerly inconsistency, but by Stupid himself.

You may recall that his commonest pastime in these situations was watching television. While Sage's dim human brain had only registered the news and the old westerns, Stupid had taken the opportunity to improve himself, and when Sage was safely snoring, Stupid would switch the channel to the educational stations. Besides picking up a lot of useful information, No-Name Stupid had taught himself to meditate, slowing his breath to an inaudible whisper. He had not only learned to control his baser urges, unleashing them only when he wished, but was discovering a whole range of strange new abilities.

But because he was, at heart, a companionable soul and had no one to share these things with, No-Name Stupid was both bored and lonely. The assorted horses, burros, and the brown mule were alright in their way, but not exactly intellectual giants.

On the bright side, the thought that he was a horse of many resources (see previous page) had sparked his imagination, giving birth to a new short poem.

Resourceful horse
The gorse, tis coarse
But t'would be worse
If from a curse
The horse was Norse
Or spoke in Morse (code)

There, thought No-Name Stupid, *not perfect, but a good work in progress.*

CHAPTER
TWENTY-NINE

eanwhile, the Nanobots were ceaselessly active, guided by their leader, Nano Prime One. Their new directive was to stop destroying forgotten machines and making more Nanobots, but instead to work with various groups and even individual beings to improve conditions everywhere. Since the whole planet, whether or not this included anything beyond Dry Gulch Canyon, was plainly out of control, the Nanobots' only assignment was to *take care of them* or (alternate interpretation) to *make them behave.* How they implemented this was up to each Nanobot to figure out for itself.

It was inevitable that some Nanobots attached themselves to the Squidren and hitched a ride back to the ship. There they created a mild annoyance, interfering with minor ship functions and, for some reason, preparing thousands of artificial sandwiches and trying to give bubble baths to the unwilling Squids. Since the Squid did not *eat* in any usual sense, and since frequent immersion in the Squidpool kept them scrupulously clean, these were misguided projects. Fairly harmless, but still a grievous waste of time and resources.

While some Nanobots set up a sort of deli and filled the Squidpool with foamy bubbles, others ransacked the computers, quickly encountering TechieSquid's report on the Alternate Universe and the Cave Wall Project. From this point, they lost discipline and began excitedly streaming through the ever-increasing holes and gaps in Halycon Sage's wall. The dawn of consciousness and a slight intellectual improvement had done nothing to diminish their desire to go everywhere and do everything.

" **O** kay, here's the game plan," said John Kennedy, testing out two of his new Earth idioms in one sentence. "We hear the reports from Four and Lol-Bey about their contacts with the two new species, then we decide which one is primary, and finally we move to the next phase of the plan. The situation is heating up!"

"First just I'd like to say"—he did the Squid equivalent of clearing his throat— "*Excellent* work on the Cave Wall Project, dear Mohammeds!" Mohammed Schmidt, Obiwan Mohammed, and Muhammad Wang Smith all looked gratified.

"Er, it's *Muhammad*, sir," said Muhammad Wang Smith, speaking softly, yet with dignity. There was a brief interval while the commander performed *The Apology Ceremony for the Spoken Misspelling of Subordinate's Name.*

"Let's have those reports now, please."

"Commander! Commander!" TechieSquid came in at a fast slither. This rudeness was unprecedented, but Kennedy was fond of TechieSquid and knew that the youngster, though sometimes thoughtless, would not commit such a breach of decorum unless something very serious had occurred.

"Yes?" All eyes turned to the young fellow.

"Well, you know how I have to be here all the time because if there isn't one of us thinking about the ship for an hour or more it will disappear? Because it's not really here at all, just a mental construct? Because we don't need it within the proximity of a planet, and it's just here to make the Earthers feel like we're proper aliens?"

"Yes, sailor, we know all this," said Kennedy with slightly exaggerated patience. (Nobody was going to mention that they couldn't have the *Squidpool* without the ship and they *really needed* the Squidpool.) "Would you come to the point, please?"

Really, this was strange and interesting. The young Squid was almost panting, which should have been impossible given his physiology.

"And you know how I've been receiving all those broadcasts, television and radio and stuff, keeping an eye on them in between visualizing the ship?"

This was growing tiresome. Several Squidiler looked at their 'watches'. (There is no way to explain in Earth terms what they actually did.) Everyone regarded him silently. If this kept up much longer, their indulgence for a young Squid who was a favorite around the ship would be exhausted, and he would be facing punishment.

"Yes?"

"*Who's broadcasting them?*"

There was a moment of stunned silence, faces blank with shock.

"Well, the Earthers, of course. The radio and T.V. broadcasts are in English, Russian, Spanish, Albanian. Who else could it be?" asked Muhammad Wang Smith, feeling as though the ground was dissolving beneath her and grasping for a foothold. But even as she spoke, she knew this was ridiculous. The senior Squidren let the young one speak for all of them since he had made the discovery.

"*But the Earthers have no tech!*" exclaimed TechieSquid. "Since our intervention with the Nanobots, they haven't been able to broadcast anything! The closest thing is the reel-to-reel Saturday night movie in Dry Creek Gulch! There's no way they could be doing this! There's only one place it could be coming from," he continued, as if all this craziness was not already enough. "The Alternate Universe!"

CHAPTER
THIRTY

The Blue and Orange Threads Converge

he Squids sat silent. This would take some contemplation, at least a day or two. They felt much as Sophie had when she discovered that her interest in the Squids' religion and language had blinded her to the fact that they had computers. Sometimes when you're focused on one thing, you just completely, absolutely, totally miss something else. Based on these two incidents, this experience does not appear to be confined to any one culture, form, or galaxy.

The Squidiler had been so flummoxed by their sudden discovery that the broadcasts were coming from the Alternate Universe that they instantly entered a multi-day contemplation, with several vanishing completely under the clear blue waters of the Squidpool.

It was TechieSquid's fault. He had *known* about the Alternate Universe, the continuing broadcasts, and the impossibility, following the Nanobots' intervention, that they could be coming from Dry Creek Gulch. He had simply failed to put the pieces together.

Somewhat bored and depressed as he was, left alone on the ship with nobody but MysterySquid for company—and MysterySquid was not much company—a renewed and dedicated focus on the work at hand had seemed the best remedy. This work was well rewarded. Through the sophisticated functions of the ship's computers, TechieSquid had discovered the Alternate Universe, hitherto known only to Halycon Sage.

He had shared the basic facts about it with Kennedy and the crew. Nothing in the Alternate Universe seemed to be filled out in any detail except the Earth, but every other asteroid, moon, planet, system, and galaxy was duplicated there as well, ready for attention and study to add definition. He had actually begun writing a memo to his superiors but had not gotten around to submitting it. It included a list of the most salient features of his discovery, which he considered interesting but not urgent.

In the Alternate Universe:

(a) There are no Nanobots.

(b) Technology still works.

(c) The United States of America has been taken over by a crazy dictator.

(d) There are whole buildings full of people who do nothing but write and study words. There are hundreds of thousands of such people, maybe millions, whereas in Dry Creek Gulch there are only three.

(e) There are also millions, maybe billions, of small children.

At this point, he was aware of the Alternate Universe as something that Halycon Sage was writing and which had assumed a sort of quasi-reality. He knew, as did the rest of the Squidiler, that this reality had split off from the original at the moment of the Nanobots' creation. *But no one had realized until now that the Alternate Reality was the source of the broadcasts.*

This meant that, in contrast to the many self-contained and derivative systems with which the Squid were familiar, its inhabitants had the ability to act, communicate, and affect others *across realities!* This was unprecedented and proved that the denizens of the Alternate Reality were at least as real as the inhabitants of Dry Creek Gulch.

TechieSquid was one of the first to recover from the surprise of this additional discovery and at once set about completing his report. He left the original matter-of-fact tone unchanged, hoping a casual competence on his part would elicit a corresponding attitude from the rest of the Squidiler, helping to erase his mistake. But he added a concluding recommendation:

<u>Conclusion</u>: The Dry Creek Gulch Project should be dropped immediately and all our attention focused on the Cave Wall Project and the Alternate Universe. Since, as everyone knows, the most powerful and highly developed individuals in any group are the small children and the grammarians, there should be plenty of partners willing and able to help us save the Two Worlds, both True Earth and its mirror world, the Alternate Universe, with profoundly positive effects on both.

He did a quick scan up and down the timeline looking for problems and anomalies. But such was his excitement over the richness and significance of this new phase that he barely noticed the multiple recurrence of two ominous phrases: "Mad Grammarians" and "Home for Delusional Grammarians." After weeks of doing nothing more exciting than trying to drown out "Ya Gotta Put on Pants," which had stuck as an earworm in his head, he was in no condition to realize the threat these words implied.

"Let's have your reports, please," said Commander Kennedy, trying again a few days later. It was time to get the plan back on track, as far as that was still appropriate. Having heard that at least one of the envoys had experienced some difficulties, he assumed an informal and consoling demeanor. These junior

Squid, and even Four, would need reassurance in the face of the developing chaos. Lol-Bey and Four stood at attention, then relaxed as he signaled at ease.

Four spoke first. "It went well, Commander. The horse is both intelligent and telepathic, and he seems like a reasonable being. I was able to update him on the situation quickly, and he has offered his help and even his friendship. I think he too was growing disillusioned with the humans."

"Excellent," said Kennedy. "And you?"

Unfortunately, Lol-Bey was unable to report a similar success. He cast his mind back to the meeting, then shared his memory telepathically with the waiting group:

Cat and Squid stood silent, looking at each other. One was a marmalade tabby, about two feet long and weighing twelve pounds. The other stood eight feet tall, shimmering deep blue shading to peacock green, weight unguessable. *Do we Squid even have weight?* he wondered yet again. And yet there seemed to be no difference in their actual sizes, in their significance as sentient beings. The cat was bigger than he looked.

Neither moved. Garnet-red eyes stared into peridot-green ones, and the green ones stared back. Neither blinked.

The Squid broke the silence first, raising several tentacles in friendship. "Hail, Stripe-ed One, may your words be always luminous!" This was a polite and ceremonial greeting from a civilization that valued words above all. For words were the vessels of Truth and Divinity, the containers of Light.

The cat sat and looked, unmoving. Lol-Bey wondered what this signified. He 'cleared his throat' (untranslatable Squid equivalent) and prepared to recite a poem, composing it on the spur of the moment, as was the custom.

> Jagged Mars-fingered drainage,
> Erudite in the extreme—Wait!
> There is no cattle where the mines is building
> And the radishes pound on, apace.

The cat's tail began to twitch. Taking this as encouragement, Lol-Bey continued, feeling his inspiration build.

> Forthright, fork-wright, builder of wingtips,
> Who built this city on rock 'n roll?
> Who calibrates the calipers?
> Optometrist, eye thyself. Aye, thyself. I, thyself.

He sat back, flushed with the victory of successful creation. There was really nothing like it!

Soundlessly, the cat turned and walked away.

A brief silence followed this revelation. John Kennedy shook his head, considering.

"Well, I don't see how you can be blamed. It is a *fine poem,* indeed! Perhaps the translation machine was malfunctioning. Or perhaps these felines have a different poetic sensibility."

The Squidren looked at each other in bafflement. Despite his youth, Lol-Bey's poems had made him known throughout the home world, as famous as Halycon Sage. It was one of the reasons he had been sent on this far-flung mission. It was assumed that no sentient being could resist his spell.

Time to change the tone, thought the Commander, shifting direction abruptly. "Here are your assignments."

The Squidiler perked up. Other than arguing about language, there was nothing they enjoyed more than really getting down to work with an alien species, and the cross-dimensional aspects made it all the better.

"Four, you seem to have a talent for diplomacy. Please initiate contact with the Orange One and see if you can have greater success than our brother here."

All the Squidren, including the Commander and Four, sent kindly glances and telepathic/energetic encouragement toward the embarrassed Lol-Bey. They wanted him to understand that anyone can make a mistake, especially in these tricky situations, and that no one was blaming him.

"Mr. Chang, you and I will enter the Alternate Universe and contact the power groups there, the children under five and the grammarians. With their help we should be able to overthrow the various dictators and institute a worldwide response to the ecological crisis.

"This effect should rebound in turn and improve conditions in Dry Gulch Canyon. I don't anticipate any difficulty in doing this. After all, there are billions of small children and grammarians in the Alternate Universe. All other individuals will surely quail at the combined powers of even a *few* of them." (*Of course* they would! Several Squidren wondered why the commander felt the need to state something so obvious.)

"Mohammeds—I mean, Mohammeds and *Muhammad*," he added, hastily correcting himself, "you keep going on the Cave Wall Project. You're doing fine work there. Sage is receptive and becoming ever more committed to the Side of Good throughout the multiverse. His intentions and heart have always been good, of course, but he has been what the Earthers called Chaotic Good in some of their games. Perhaps under *our* influence, he may become a bit more disciplined."

It may be of passing interest that a small group of wandering Chilidians caught the last part of this summation. They had been monitoring the situation on Earth for quite some time.

"Halycon Sage, disciplined!" they chortled, clacking their great green claws in pure enjoyment. They couldn't wait to share the hilarity of this assumption and its probable consequences with the Lava Cone back home. Truly, the Squidren in their earnest efforts to save the multiverse were unequalled for unintentional comedy.

Perhaps something of their mirth penetrated the consciousness of Commander Kennedy, who had been chosen partly for his extraordinary sensitivity to thought waves and cross-currents in the space-time continuum.

"Or, wait a moment," he corrected. "Mohammeds, why don't you come with us for the time being? Sage seems to be doing well on his own. We'll take the short route through the cave wall into the Alternate Universe. Our goal is to contact our natural allies, the grammarians and small children, as quickly as possible. *All* of them, if we can."

TechieSquid wondered why Kennedy had thought it necessary to mention natural allies. The importance of grammarians and small children was surely known to every wriggling Squidlet. *But perhaps,* he thought, *the Commander is preserving the record, to be understood by non-Squidren who may someday read his words.*

Suddenly, and most unexpectedly, there came a disturbance. Kennedy heard shouting and scuffling, and immediately the room was filled with sentient beings at approximately the human level. A tall man, apparently the leader, approached a random Squid. He seemed highly agitated.

"What exactly is *going on* here? What did you people *do?* Do you know that you've split the universe in half and created *another one? And who in the Name of God is Halycon Sage?*"

CHAPTER

THIRTY-ONE

Things had calmed down a bit aboard the squidship. Four had gotten the Nanobots out of everyone's hair (so to speak) by the brilliant expedient of convincing them to give bubble baths to *each other*. They were enjoying the experience. This had entailed chasing the zi out of the Squidpool, but it was time for them to come out anyway as they were beginning to wrinkle.

She had also provided all the visitors and participating Squid with sandwiches, hot tea, bowls of water, dried algae with bugs, or little bowls of light depending on their needs. There was really nobody like Four when it came to diplomacy.

Various humans, Squidren, and other odd creatures were distributed about the main cabin and adjoining areas. (This part of the ship was designed on the Open Plan.) Something that looked like a green snake with red spots but wearing a sort of pith helmet flowed into the room on delicate wings. It nodded politely.

There was a kind of Ape-Thing too, which also nodded politely, taking a seat on the commander's bunk. The commander hoped it had washed recently.

"So, how did you find us?" John Kennedy asked conversationally. He was actually enjoying himself. This new craziness provided some relief from the unrelenting pressures of command and the constant feeling he had hit a brick wall. New game pieces were being dealt. Perhaps there would be new solutions as well.

"It was this Halycon Sage," replied Rupert Griffin. "He wrote to me."

"How did he get a letter to you?" inquired Kennedy mildly.

"Now that, sir, is a good question! It came through a hole in my wall. I can only conclude that he transferred it through time and space by some method unknown to me. Though I am not unacquainted with matter transfer and even the transfer of living beings."

"You'd never seen it done like this?" interrupted TechieSquid somewhat rudely. The older Squidren and others made allowances. Of course the youngster was excited. A new chapter in time and space was being revealed.

"You see," continued Griffin, "my team here and I represent the core of a company called Unvirtual Time Travel . . ."

"UVTT: We *take* you there!" added the spotted snake. "And it's not a company, sir, it's an agency. Remember? *An agency*." The snake was head of public relations and for some reason was touchy about this matter.

His unobtrusive assistant, the black-haired, blue-eyed Miss O'Connell, tried to calm him as usual. The snake fancied himself an artist and was offended when the fine crafting of his words and images was violated.

"You're right that there is something unusual about this Sage," replied Kennedy. "His mind works in a strange way, and he travels between dimensions, usually without realizing he's doing it. Of course that's not at all unheard of, though not terribly common. What *is* unusual is that he seems able to affect the rest of us as he travels, again, with no idea he is doing so. That's what gave us the idea . . ."

"Of using him to save the Earth!" finished TechieSquid in triumph. Four shook her head at him reprovingly. Really, someone would need to speak with the lad.

"Exactly," chimed in John Chang, earning a faint and ladylike snort from the Squidress for aiding and abetting bad manners.

"There was a brilliant and apparently autistic scientist named Preisczech, and we noticed the perfect congruence between his attributes and those of Halycon Sage. We saw that they matched like two halves of a clamshell, each compensating for the other. Each was a damaged genius; together they were an invincible power for the good."

Kennedy took up the thread again. "So, we introduced them, and the rest is history. With the support and friendship of Sage, Preisczech invented the Nanobots, the Nanobots destroyed all modern technology, and Bob's your uncle!"

The commander had evidently gotten carried away with his study of Earth idioms and discovered some mostly forgotten ones, adding a further layer of confusion to the tasks of translation and interpretation. TechieSquid hit the On-board Translation Machine a smart *thwack,* assuming it was malfunctioning again. While the Squidren were reliably telepathic, they sometimes used technology as a substitute or supplement, depending on the race they were dealing with.

"Only instead of healing the Earth," mused Griffin, "You merely walled off *one* reality, the one you had altered, and created a second one that went on as before. Of course alternate realities are not unusual, but there are some unique features about this one, or rather this set of two."

"What do you mean?" asked Four. Her seniority was high enough that this was not considered interrupting.

Griffin started naming the issues, indicating them one by one on his rather elegant fingers. "One. The reality that has been walled off is the *one containing the instigators* of the split. Usually, it would be the second and subsidiary reality that was walled off.

"Two. Beings within the sealed planet are still able to affect the split-off location and are doing so at a great rate and with a variety of results and motives. You charming Squidren, at least two humans, a cat, and some things called Nanobots are all doing so. This is very, very unusual, I might say unprecedented.

"Three. There appears to be a wall within a wall. At least that is my first impression, but it is really difficult to say whether anything at all of the original Earth remains outside of Dry Creek Gulch. The town may have been isolated during the split (what you call the Event) while the rest of your planet carries on. Or the town may be all that is left, floating in a void.

"Four. You may notice that I said *two* humans were intervening. One, of course, is Halycon Sage. The other, name unknown, has come into our reality, gone back in time, and created the most appalling mess. I am here in answer to Sage's impassioned plea about a certain fictional dog, but we of Unvirtual Time Travel are also here to join tentacles with you and see if there is anything to be done."

In this room, on this Squidship, there were bodies of various shapes and colors and a variety of languages, cultures, psychic abilities, talents, and levels of expertise and intelligence. But at this moment, their hearts were one. They understood each other well.

An intricate minuet
Subtle and elegant
These are our watchwords
This is the tenor
Of our thoughts
The patterns, the patterns!
This is why we live.

A Poem, by Karima Vargas Bushnell

PART FIVE

THE APOTHEOSIS

WHEREIN the Green Thread is unveiled and illumined as we attempt to save the planet. "The earth is green and beautiful, and God has made you His caretakers over it."[4]

---

4   Hadith of the Prophet Muhammad, s.a.w.s. The initials at the end are a sort of technical Muslim thing. They stand for, "Salallahu 'aleyhi wa salam," meaning "Peace and blessing be upon him." Something similar is used for Jesus and others. People also sometimes use p.b.u.h. for the English translation, or use a tiny image of calligraphy. (The latter looks very pretty.)

CHAPTER
THIRTY-TWO

The walls between Sage's reality and his imagination had become thin, and both worlds were leaking back and forth all over the place. Sage was not aware of this. Following the example of the first enterprising Nanobot who had climbed through one of the cave holes, both Nanobots and Squid were pouring into the Alternate Reality. While this began with the two holes in the cave wall, it wasn't long until time and space leaks were appearing everywhere.

One Squid went back and forth through a hollow tree, and another had discovered a portal in the back of an old wardrobe in one of the disused houses[24]. Some didn't even bother with these devices but just stepped across dimensions, imagining themselves into the other place, which received them with a thin, stretching feeling, followed by a popping sound as their bodies were displaced by warm desert air.

The Nanobots had been invented as a unit with a single purpose. Preisczech could have told you that giving them individuation, volition, and free will was a really bad idea, but he had could not have anticipated the catastrophic effect of the Red Button, let alone the intervention and participation of the Squid.

Preisczech, Jenny, and Stupid had been gone for weeks, exploring and mapping the Perimeter Wall, and now after the double stress of his misadventure at the dinner and his involvement in the daring rescue, Preisczech was again barricaded in his house. Thus, any check his scientific genius might have applied to the whole ridiculous situation was not to be had.

The Squidren's first move upon finding themselves in the Alternate Universe, in the same country that Sage was writing about, was to contact the most important, influential, and powerful members of the human community there. This was standard procedure, agreed upon by most civilizations of time and space travelers, though there were dissenting views.

The result was a spate of reports about the eccentric imaginings taking place within the two groups contacted. In the case of the most powerful group, which the Squid knew to be small children, the sudden appearance in their childish conversation of giant walking, talking, blue green or purpley blue squid who wanted them to save the world was put down to their young imaginations.

The consequences for the other group, English and other language teachers and anybody who made a study of words, were far more serious. They were summarily fired and packed off to newly reopened mental institutions, which welcomed them with open arms. There, they babbled about alien squid and cross-dimensional time travel till the doctors, nurses, and other staff grew tired of listening to them and gave them something to calm them down. Hence, this peculiar scene witnessed by that quintessential feline dimension hopper, Fatty Lumpkin.

The orange cat sat on the windowsill of the mental institution, swishing his striped tail. No one could explain how he got there, or where he went when he disappeared, or how he seemed able to come back and leave again at will. But this sill in the dayroom, exposed to light and with the illusion of fresh air, was his favorite spot.

This place and others like it had been doing a land-office business since the ordinary tensions of post-modern life and the outrages of the developing dictatorship had been exacerbated by many, many reports of giant, luminous, blue, walking squid that talked. Nobody much believed these reports since the main adult group affected appeared to be teachers and professors of languages and anyone else who made a study of words, be it phonetics, linguistics, oratory, style, or grammar. This merely reinforced the already widespread impression that these people were crazy.

The other group reporting Squid encounters were children under five, and of course no one paid any attention to *them*.

The cat looked around at the semi-comatose bodies slumped in wheelchairs, the abandoned food trays, the unwatched television transmitting nonsense. He made a little poem in his head:

Haldol, Demerol
Swishy-tail and Bumpkin
Too many drugs in here
Says Old Fatty Lumpkin

Some of the Mad Grammarians, as they were euphoniously but inaccurately dubbed by the Alternate Universe press, were more docile than their fellows and so were not subject to the overwhelming drug treatment. These managed to issue some very odd, apparently channeled publications, which were pretty much ignored by everybody. One example:

From *The Squidly Times* [Date Line]

A terrible thing has happened since *The Book of Lighted Squid* has come to public knowledge, and some rowdies in *a state which shall here be nameless* decided that this had something to do with barbeque, bought a lot of beer and . . . to continue is too painful, but there is some hope that, due to intervention by some right-thinking citizens, the several Squid in question escaped the worst consequences. We, the Editors, prefer to think so, anyway. But the incident has given fuel (no pun intended) to the unwarranted, offensive, and even blasphemous movement toward rechristening the Holy Book *The Book of Squidly Light*. Such rash and unwarranted innovations must of course be resisted. That should go without saying. Even though I just said it.

"We live in squidly times."
— Editor, *Squidly Times*

Since nobody had ever heard of either *The Book of Lighted Squid* or *The Book of Squidly Light*, this article in English Teachers' Quarterly was universally ignored, put down as just one more example of the inexplicable insanity of the times, which was probably just as well.

With all these things happening, Halycon Sage was still absent from domestic and communal activities. It was taking him a lot of time to write all this nonsense.

The Shadowy Man was standing unobserved in the only shadowy place in the main room of the Canis Fidelis. He had a way of melting into the dark so others overlooked him. It was a trick he had learned.

The bar was such a locus of community life that he visited it several times a week to watch what was going on and see what information he could pick up. After all, this was where he had overheard Preisczech trying to tell the dim-witted Dirty Dog Gang about the Nanobots so long ago. He alone had understood. It was possible that equally valuable information awaited him now.

He scanned the occupants. A few local characters, but nobody of real interest. Anthony (f.k.a. Buzzard of the Dog Gang) and the Iraqi family who now lived with him—*there* was a weird juxtaposition if you liked—were at a table playing some foolish game with Nuri. Jenny and Preisczech were slow dancing to the suddenly working jukebox, a sight to make anyone sick. Ratbone, Sophie, and Vasselschnauzer were having some sort of literary argument. Yawn. Some other insignificant townspeople were doing insignificant things. It was looking like a wasted trip.

The Shadowy Man walked to the door, still silent, still unobserved. *I'm very big with shadows,* he thought, involuntarily quoting a theatrical production he despised for its popularity, as he despised pretty much everything[25]. He stood a moment near the door, scanning the notice board. He stopped. Sophie's first posting stared him in the face, together with its one responding comment. *How had he missed this?* The Squid have computers! *The Squid have computers.* THE SQUID HAVE COMPUTERS.

Sometime later, in the Other Cave—the Cave of Darkness—an odd assortment of creatures was once again assembled. The leader, of course, was the Shadowy Man. Sitting, standing, or floating around him were several other beings: his detestable side-kick Spiffy, Skull of the Dirty Dog Gang, a few obscure Fifth Street Mofos, and the Apocalypse Zombie, now known to us, though to no one else, as Edgar.

There were also two Squidiler, and they were rather odd, even for Squid. One was unusually silent, hanging back in the shadows. The other seemed to shift, appearing at one moment as a tall, blue-purple Squid, at another as a beautiful human woman, dressed in sparkling garments and veils of midnight blue. Both her forms were luminescent, and these shifts were subtle and not noticed by everyone. It was quite possible that some saw her as a Squid, others as a woman, and almost no one as some creature containing both.

"The time has come," said the Shadowy Man impressively, "and it is necessary for you to know something of my plan. Some of you are aware that there are working computers aboard the squidship. For those of you that are not, let me inform you now. There are working computers aboard the squidship."

He stopped a moment, nearly losing his thread. This business of being a supervillain was apt to shade into self-parody if not carefully controlled. "Our mission is to board the ship and remove the computers so that only I have access to them. Only *I*, in all of Dry Creek Gorge! Only *I, in all the world!*"

The phrase "drunk with power" floated through his mind. *Get a grip*, he told himself, *we don't want this to turn out like last time.* "That is, *we*, my friends. *We* will have access to the computers." He looked around in satisfaction.

"Why?" asked Skull. "Who cares?" *All I want is a damned drink. Computers were boring and pointless* before *the Event. Why should they be any better now?*

The Shadowy Man repressed a sigh. Some of his minions were not too bright.

"It doesn't matter. You'll understand later. For now, here's the plan: We board the Squidship. We overpower anyone who tries to resist us. We remove the computers along with their power source and take them. If this proves impossible, we open them where they are and copy all the files, destroying them behind us—again, if that is possible. We also read, scan, copy, whatever we can do, any documents or recordings that are lying around. I am informed that only a skeleton crew of one or two is awake and aware at any given time, outside of meetings.

"Having accomplished these things, we will leave. After, perhaps, inflicting a bit of extra damage on the ship and the Squidren. Inflicting some pain." He smiled. "Sparky, perhaps you would like to use your fire-starting talents in some way."

Sparky, who had been drifting, perked up.

Oh man, thought Big D, *I knew I shouldn't of let him get involved with this. This sucks! But I can control him, as long as I stick close. For sure I can. And look how well he did at the barbecue!*

"Let's go," said the Shadowy Man.

And they did.

CHAPTER
THIRTY-THREE

asel Vasselschnauzer was not a happy camper. While he had never been noted for his sunny temper—his petulance, irritability, and general viciousness toward the unfortunate authors he critiqued had been the stuff of legend—since the Event he had been remarkably agreeable. Companionable, even. But not anymore.

The secret of his personality changes was this: Vasselschnauzer had been raised with money, but not with love. He had grown from a superior little horror in short pants into an impeccably dressed young student whose wit was a deadly sword, waiting to ambush his blithely unconscious professors. Because the kid was *smart*, and a hell of a writer.

Though he had what used to be called "a taking style"—when he chose, his dormitory bedtime stories could be spell-binding—he did not have enough empathy or compassion to sustain his interest in any character beyond the length of a short story.

Thus, he became a critic, scourge of the New York literati, loved by none, respected by some, feared by nearly all. While he began with a certain amount of integrity, this was quickly eroded by the conviction that he was smarter than everyone else and that ninety-nine percent of them were not worth bothering about anyway.

By the time the pre-Event scenario began unfolding, he had taken to deciding his attitude toward new authors with a dart board, eyes closed, sealing their fates with the red-feathered dart of life or the black-feathered dart of death. In truth, he had become more interested in the idiosyncratic lists of likes and dislikes in his weekly column, "What We Like and Why" than in any book or author.

Opinion was divided as to whether Vasselschnauzer was heterosexual, homosexual, bisexual, or asexual. The truth was, he was none of these. He was merely bored.

He had never had a relationship with anyone from his mother onward that was worth a bucket of spit, and he saw no reason to expend his energies on such matters. Until the time when he appears in the first Chronicle, Basel Vasselschnauzer had never loved, never *been* loved, never even had a friend.

His fantastic dartboard skills had earned him some admirers in Great Britain and Ireland, and before his eccentricity and bad temper had eclipsed his initially fine critical sense, parts of the literary world had held him in awe. But no one had ever been permitted to draw near. Those who tried were chased away with waspish words that lingered long in their memories, little pools of agonizing embarrassment to be revealed only to the most expensive therapists.

The last few months before the Event changed all that. His acts of critical irresponsibility having passed all bounds, he was sent away by the one person with any power over him, the man who could distribute or refuse to distribute his syndicated column. His mission was the king of all wild goose chases: to find mysterious author Halycon Sage, a man whose whereabouts, origins, heredity, habits, face, and voice were equally unknown. Basel had compared his task to catching the wind in a butterfly net. *Nobody* knew anything about Halycon Sage.

Venturing beyond the bounds of civilization into the wild lands west of New Jersey, he eventually ended up in Dry Creek Gulch, where a few matter-of-fact words changed his life.

"Come on, Katzenpauzer, let's blow this pop stand," she had said, or words to that effect, after telling him with equal casualness that she knew where to find Halycon Sage. And he was so surprised that he did it. He went along.

No one had ever talked to him like this, casually assuming his participation in a collaborative enterprise, an adventure, even. Nobody had ever, even in his boyhood, treated him like *one of the gang*. His meeting with Ruby had changed everything.

Now Ruby was too busy for him, Sage had vanished again, and the others he had begun to grow close to seemed to be pulling away. Without Sage, who was a kind of Basel-whisperer, his tendency to whine and complain about everything from the fit of his boots to the weight of his backpack had alienated the other bow hunters. Since Sage's latest disappearance, Anthony/Buzzard had become a competent leader and pretty much taken over the group. And Anthony, also raised in wealth, had little use for Vasselschnauzer.

It was just the same as always. Nobody cared. Nobody gave a damn. And where were his green silk cushions, his black marble bar, his gin and vodka, his oysters and caviar—all the things that had formerly led him to believe his life was happy? They were gone. But now that he had experienced actual friendship and belonging, they would probably not have been enough.

Dammit all anyway, thought Basel. He was sitting in the back room behind the bar at the Dirty Dog, a place where he had once been tied after being kidnapped and from which he had courageously escaped in the defining act of his life.

There was something a little funny about that room in the Dirty Dog. It had some of the same quality as Halycon Sage's cave. Things were not always where you left them, or they appeared suddenly out of nowhere, and the space seemed to expand and contract, to darken and lighten depending on the needs of the occupants.

Basel sat back against the wall—dear God, he had become a *floor sitter*, could there be any greater indignity?—and picked up *The Blessing Way*, the first Chee and Leaphorn novel by Tony Hillerman. If these were any good, he could distract himself from reality for quite some time because there was a whole stack of them.

There was a sudden scrabbling sound in the corner. The orange and white striped cat who was quite a town character was back there, scratching at the pages of an open book. Perhaps he was trying to do his business in there, mistaking the book for a cat box. Basel's low opinion of others' intelligence was not confined to humans. Though he wasn't sure about these Squid. It might be worth cultivating a few of them, seeing if they had any literary sensibilities. Now there was a new idea! The thought flared briefly in his mind, then quickly subsided into the listless boredom that was becoming habitual with him.

He looked around again. The cat continued scratching at the book, his movements assuming a desperate air. He looked at Basel pointedly, almost as if he wanted to communicate. But he still seemed to be trying to dig a hole in the book. Basel looked away. Stupid cat.

He drifted off into some pointless fantasy between sleep and waking, too ill-focused even to remember. Then into deeper sleep. When he next awakened, something was nudging his hand, a small nose and a hard, silky head. It was the cat, who had somehow pushed or carried the book to Vasselschnauzer's side. Well, that was not so extraordinary. It was a small book.

The cat looked up in mute appeal. Basel gazed back in bafflement. Absurd as it was, anyone would think the cat was asking him to do something about the book, but what it was he could not divine. While his intelligence was massive, it was focused in one direction only, toward the creation, assimilation, and evaluation of words. In other areas, he may have been somewhat lacking.

The two continued to look at each other.

Turn the page, thought the cat, slowing his thoughts and increasing their intensity. *Hear me, human. Turn the page.*

Basel looked a moment more, engaging with the enigmatic green eyes. For a moment he almost understood. Surely that cat wanted . . . No. He shook off the foolish fantasy and looked away. When next he looked, the cat was gone.

"**Y**ou again?" asked Halycon Sage agreeably. He had been ready for a bit of company. "Let's see if I can find a piece of baloney for you." But he was not quick enough. One moment the cat was sitting against the wall. The next he was gone, and where he had disappeared to was once again a mystery. *Another* one. Also, there seemed to be a vaguely Squidish form in the corner. Sage rubbed his eyes.

"Stick a fork in me, I'm done," he mumbled. It was time for a nap.

CHAPTER
THIRTY-FOUR

omehow, Sage kept coming back to the idea of writing a romance novel. *Not*, he hastily assured himself, the kind of semi-erotic extravaganza he had contemplated for about two seconds until he realized how the real Ruby would react if he ever shared their private moments. And he really had no other experience to draw on, considering his still-lingering amnesia problems.

But the idea of a love story kept recurring. Perhaps it was because he was *missing* Ruby. Sage, essentially a modest person, was becoming more and more convinced that she would never want him back, and the longer he stayed away in the cave, the more he felt like Rip Van Winkle. Or maybe like those Seven Sleepers that Abdurraheem had told him about, guys who thought they'd been asleep for "a day, or part of a day," but it turned out to be hundreds of years. At least they had their dog to keep them company, and in the end, they all went to heaven, the dog too. Sage had liked that story. Right now he could have *used* a dog. Face it, it was *lonely* in here.

Suddenly, he had another thought, one that eclipsed the romance novel with a brilliant burst of unrelated inspiration. He had written most politely to Griffin, and Griffin had not answered him. To be fair, it was quite likely that his message had gone astray. If you write a letter and stick it into some interdimensional hole in the wall, there's no knowing where it might come out.

Sage had been counting on the fact that, since he was apparently writing this whole mess, steering it as it were, the power of his intent would be enough to guide the letter to its intended recipient. But he really had no idea how any of this worked. What was under his control and what wasn't. Whether or not the Squids or anyone else were creating cross-currents with their own intentions and manipulations. And whether the whole shooting match was imaginary or, as he had begun to suspect, it was all frighteningly real.

As usual, his mind had gone from tangent to tangent, like a jazz musician too far out on a limb from the original melody, and it was now completely out in left field. He brought it back sternly.

Here was the thing: it might be that Griffin had never gotten his message, or that he had lived years ago and was no longer available. Sage had no way of knowing. It seemed more likely, however, that Griffin *had* received the message and was simply ignoring him. Which was just impolite.

In any case, since he had received no answer to his heartfelt plea on behalf of one poor imaginary dog, it was high time he took the initiative and did something about it. After all, he too was a writer!

Sage assumed a cross-legged position, faced the mysterious wall, and set about visualizing a large and loyal black Labrador retriever. If this didn't work, he could try writing his wishes. Bringing the dog here would be better for both of them: the dog would be resurrected to a world of food and love and places to run (assuming they ever got out of the cave), and Sage would finally have some company.

"Come on, doggie, doggie, doggie," breathed Halycon Sage. *"Come to papa."*

How history *does* repeat itself, especially when time travel is involved. One might almost imagine that one were trapped in an ever-repeating loop. So, once again, TechieSquid was bored. Everything that could be checked had *been* checked, and his strange combination of advanced alien technology and natural abilities—most of which would be considered psychic or paranormal on Earth—had been set to catch any new developments.

There was a stack of reports, hilariously printed on paper: information on the Alternate Universe, Unvirtual Time Travel, interdimensional breakthroughs, Halycon Sage, and other matters. These papers had been ordered up by the ever-conscientious Commander Kennedy and awaited delivery to him at the proper time. TechieSquid had done what was needed to prepare them but had been too bored to engage with them on any thoughtful level. He really would have preferred getting out on the planet for a breath of air.

The zi had still not been allowed out—though a few had ventured—for fear they would shock the Earthers, but they didn't have it so rough. The nanobots were given another harmless task and the zi were back in the Squidpool swimming happily, zonked out of their minds on the blissfully psychedelic water. It was good for them, too! When they came out, their strength would be quadrupled. They were currently enjoying their returned companion's tales of the barbecue, even going so far as to act them out.

TechieSquid briefly considered trying to draw out MysterySquid. If he could get him (her? zi?) to converse, to speculate, to get angry, to show joy or embarrassment or to react in any way, it would be a red-letter day. But he had tried this before, and it was pretty much hopeless. You could hardly even tell that MysterySquid was alive, and MysterySquid never really did or said anything. MysterySquid *observed*.

TechieSquid sighed and went into the Nanobots' new galley for a bowl of light. *A light snack,* he thought, *ha ha ha ha ha.*

"BOO!" shouted the Apocalypse Zombie, emerging from a broom closet (Squid equivalent). His lopsided, lumpy, half-shaven, hideously white-patched face looked even worse than usual in the sunlight/starlight blue luminescence, the radiant shimmer that filled the ship.

TechieSquid did something never done by a Squid in recorded history. Perhaps he had spent too much time monitoring Earth's entertainment broadcasts, so that they were beginning to affect his very being. He fainted dead away.

"C'mon in, boys," said the Zombie to the team.

The Stetson Black Team, the whole horror show of unsuccessful gangsters, jealous former computer hackers, the greedy, the lazy, the frightened, and the unloving, dim bulbs from every segment of the new society flowed into the ship from the weird broom closet portal. Followed by their mentor and their darling, who would eventually betray them. Only one, Big D, had some degree of honor and positive purpose, the wish to protect Sparky the fire-setter and mitigate the damage he could not help doing.

When TechieSquid awoke and examined the psychic trails the creatures had left, he found that only this one human had left a trail of goodness. But otherwise, what he found dismayed him. While the computers were undamaged, all the information in them had clearly been copied, and the stack of papers was gone. MysterySquid was gone too, but that one was so characterless that his/her/zi's comings and goings were hardly noticed by TechieSquid or anyone else.

Before reporting this latest disaster to Commander Kennedy, TechieSquid made a brief visit to the zi in the psychedelic Squidpool. They had awakened and were throwing some kind of party. *Thank God*, thought TechieSquid, *the zi were just fine.*

The Shadowy Man was well pleased. While he had been unable to steal the computers or render them unusable by the Squid, he had found something beyond his expectations. He had found UVTT's time travel technology.

He had also seen the report on the Cave Wall Project and realized that he could access the Alternate Universe through the wall of Sage's cave. Combining the two, he could do whatever he wanted to the creative, sensible, sane, proactive, and utterly disgusting world of the Alternate Universe. Ever since he had first become aware of it through the boring old pre-UVTT time and space travel technology that let you "*see* there, but never *be* there," it had been driving him nuts.

The human beings there had finally caught on to Divide and Conquer and were no longer fooled, refusing its blandishments. The different groups and nations were working together to do all the things that obviously needed doing: heading off the worst climate disasters (though this had gone too far for certainty or complacency), getting the world fed without resorting to chemicals that destroyed both health and land, preserving or even recreating animal species, moving to green energy, and educating children in ways that brought out their intelligence, kindness, and creativity—those most important resources of all.

The indigenous communities around the world were finally getting the respect they deserved, along with great thanks for keeping the vision alive while the world was insane. Young people leapt from their beds in the morning with purpose and excitement, sensing that their skills, talents, and ideas were desperately needed and immensely valued. Every child was precious!

War was almost wiped out. A few small groups of barbarians here and there were still hacking away at each other, but in general, the world had passed them by and they were looked at with pity for their atavistic tendencies.

While art, literature, music, dance, and drama flourished, and while they had not disappeared into some cookie-cutter, Communist-style rah rah, there was a lot less of the *Life is Pointless, Look at Me* school in *all* the arts.

The Shadowy Man did not approve of any of this, and now he could finally do something about it. While he was a little disappointed there'd been no chance to make Sparky torch the ship—this would have been entertaining and left both Sparky and Big D wracked with guilt for decades—this small concession to the sudden return of the Squidren from town was *nothing* compared to the havoc he could wreak on the namby-pamby, politically correct, eco-gooey morons on the other side of the barrier now that he could finally, finally get his hands on them.

Reality was in play, the outcome depending on actions and decisions about to be made in what would become the past. The kaleidoscope shifts, now this reality, now that one. Back and forth, back and forth. Steady . . . steady . . . Excellent!

⟳

Sophie was so happy, and all the other kids were too! They positively *skipped* to school, and they were teenagers, for God's sake! She saw a neighbor boy across the way and gave him a big wave, to which he responded.

He was working on the ecology; she was working on animal cell reclamation, preparatory to bringing back some of the extinct species. Of course she was not doing this by herself, but she was contributing her small part, and it was a *real* part, a real contribution. She was walking and the boy was catching the bus, as their specialized project areas lay in different directions. They would all meet up again later.

"STEM, STEM, STEM," she sang, making up a little chant. "STEAM, STEAM, STEAM," she amended it. Science, technology, engineering, ART, and math. She had to include art, or her friend Layla, who was an artist (a different Layla? Maybe, maybe not) would kill her. Not in the literal sense, of course.

She skipped again. She was so lucky to be studying under the guidance of Professor Preisczech!

The teenagers sat in the classroom. Only half of them came on any sort of regular basis. Their eyes were glazed with boredom as the teacher, also bored to extinction, was preparing them for another test. What did it *matter?* No one here actually cared about anything that was happening, including the teacher. Nobody's interest was engaged, and nobody's goal was aligned with the stated goal on which the hour was being spent.

The teacher's goal was to get this over with, get back to her apartment, and ultimately get a paycheck, for which she could not be blamed. It would allow her to *stay* in her apartment instead of being kicked out into the street, as so many were. The goal of the students was simply to get the hell out of this hell hole, as soon, and for as long, as possible. That was all.

The other half of the students have probably just stayed home, or else they're out contributing to the opium crisis, thought Sophie. *Or actually, more likely,* her dismal thoughts continued, *the police and soldiers have taken them. So many homes and classrooms and hospitals raided, so many gone.* Her friend Layla, the artist, was not here, she noticed. Her friend Layla was from Iraq.

Sophie felt the tears welling up in her eyes yet again. Unfortunately for her, she was still watching the news. The dictator's smug face was everywhere, you could not avoid it. The government was selling off the beautiful national parks, opening them up to fracking, oil drilling and mining, raising the prices for visitors to the ones that were left so that poor and ordinary people could not afford them. After the previous interior secretaries had worked so hard to open them to everybody, encouraging everyone to experience and protect the wilderness!

The dictator was insulting another dictator, who was insulting him back. Like babyish schoolyard bullies, they were threatening each other with nuclear weapons. *Perhaps they'll use them and just put us all out of our misery*, thought Sophie, with uncharacteristic despair.

CHAPTER
THIRTY-FIVE

he Universe(s) swung crazily between opposite alternatives. And why was that, my children, *why?* Listen, Best Beloved, and you shall hear.

Halycon Sage was still in his cave, and all ideas of time, space, and reality were gone. He did not even seem to eat any longer. He was simply there, witnessing, seeing pictures and words on the wall, reading them, and writing. He had given up hope of ever getting back to Ruby or Dry Gulch Canyon, or of ever getting out at *all*, really.

Some of his visions were blissful, sane, and beautiful. Others were mad and hellish. He thought he saw God once, and God told him it was going to be alright. He trusted this completely for the moment, but he wasn't able to hold on to the feeling. Time and space wheeled crazily in a drunken minuet, swinging from one possibility to the next. He simply waited, taking it all down.

One day, or one moment, or one millennium after a timeless time, he saw a shadow moving in the corner. It was a man, but barely a man, more like some kind of stick figure, not really filled out. Well, the body and so forth were filled out alright, but it was an *emotional or spiritual* stick figure, not really filled out with love, empathy, wisdom, and compassion, as humans were meant to be. Although, in its cold emptiness, it thought itself very, very intelligent. The mindprint of this person reminded Sage of someone, but he couldn't think who. It was as though he had encountered this energy before.

Then the thing slipped into one of the many dimensional holes that now covered the wall like Swiss cheese and was gone. This man, or whatever he was, had gone into the Alternate Universe. Sage felt sorry for it.

The Shadowy Man sat triumphantly on some undefined object in the Alternate Universe—as in Theatre of the Absurd, he felt no need to fill it in or define it as a chair, a stool or a big rock—and thought about what to do next.

The problem was obviously the president. *That* was what had to be fixed. A man of strong opinions, he was loved by many including, apparently, a little bird that had once landed on his podium. He said what he meant, which was abnormal behavior for a politician. This had been a shock to everybody until they adjusted.

What was worse was that he was smart, not crazy, and not just out for himself. He had good intentions, and he really thought it was pretty stupid to just destroy everything for no particular reason. And he had pulled the people together, getting them all rowing in the same direction.

When he did not know something, and there were many areas, like foreign policy, where his experience was weak, he would call in an expert, a really brilliant, experienced and well-intentioned expert who *also* thought it was stupid to just destroy everything for no particular reason.

He had won by a landslide because he made sense and everyone loved him. Well, not everyone, but enough. He could draw a crowd of 60,000 at an hour's notice. So, he had been elected. This whole situation was the Shadowy Man's nightmare.

Thus, the first obvious thing was to take down this president. It might not even be necessary to do anything else. That might be enough all by itself.

He could give him a heart attack or make somebody shoot him. That would be easy enough. He smiled to himself. Now that he had the time travel technology from UVTT and the Squid, all he needed to do was go back and make sure, by a combination of circumstances, that this man did not get elected. He would have to balance the different forces against each other, placing them just right.

There was a *woman* who wanted to be president, subtle and clever, with a lifetime of experience. She was loved by some, hated by others. She was one factor that could be important. The two main political parties, other parties, other nations—so many opportunities! And if he found the right substitute, the just-right president instead of the wrong one, it might truly be unnecessary to do anything else.

The Shadowy man shivered, annoyed with himself. He was not annoyed with his plan, which was perfect, but he was annoyed with the tone and tenor of his thoughts because they sounded exactly like the thoughts of Halycon Sage, those fragmented and childish constructions of the obvious, like building blocks made of one-syllable words. He shuddered again. This was apparently some contagion he had acquired in passing through the cave, and doubtless it was merely temporary.

The man he found was perfect. A failed millionaire, inheritor of a large fortune which, by dint of a great deal of cheating and manipulation, he had managed to parlay into an amount smaller than would have been yielded by a well-advised investment portfolio. A foul-mouthed loudmouth, a braggart, an unattractive abuser of women, drawing them inexplicably with money alone or with the promise of a cheap, glitzy fame, a pointless condition of celebrity, what one man had described by saying, "Everyone will be famous for fifteen minutes." A situation where people who did nothing and were not even entertaining were 'famous for being famous'.

This world, this view of reality, was dear to the Shadowy Man's heart. Before the Event, he had done a great deal to promote this worldview, had, in fact, been one of its major proponents.

This man was the perfect candidate, and the Shadowy Man had the expertise and the tools, combining his own cleverness and experience with all he had acquired from the Squidren and Unvirtual Time Travel, to get him where he needed to be. It would take years, but time meant nothing now. He could even go back and get the guy through college. Then a television career—as a game show host, perhaps. But all these details could be sorted out later. There was infinite time to plan this chess game, to make sure the result was correct.

"Good day, sir," said the Shadowy Man, approaching the large, awkward figure. "How would you like to be President of the United States?"

CHAPTER

THIRTY-SIX

Karima Vargas Bushnell, Alternate Universe "owner" of The Cat Fatty Lumpkin, was remembering that she had gotten his name from the Tolkien book, though she did not remember quite how or why. The imaginary author wondered why such an elegant creature should be stuck with such a stupid name.

One day it came to her: The cat was an *attorney!* He was F. Atty. Lumpkin, Esq. Now it all made sense: his style, his behavior, the charming way he communicated with her, mostly getting her to do whatever he wanted while making her feel that he was doing her a favor.

Sage too was thinking, always an interesting process. He thought again about writing the love story. Long forgotten by everyone were the days—only months ago really—when literary critics worldwide had hung on his every word. His sensational novels were tiny, quarter-page things with one or two characters, or maybe none at all.

Somehow a bit of length and complexity had developed, perhaps through his own complex interactions with Preisczech, Ruby, and even Basel Vasselschnauzer. The next giant step, trembling on the lip of actuality (*on the trembling lip of actuality? . . . verging on the trembling lip of actuality?*), would be to have characters who *interacted with each other.*

A love story was surely the most intense and interesting kind of interaction. Well, besides the western. And the detective story. Or the spy novel. Or a good legal thriller, or sci fi.

He brushed these thoughts away. He felt that there was a problem with the writing of a romance, and it was coalescing in his mind from a kind of vapor into a denser cloud of awareness that would presently let down the rain of realization.

Breathe . . . breathe . . .

Okay, here was the problem. To be interesting, a love story would need a conflict, at least if it were longer that one paragraph. Now, one kind of conflict was the personality conflict—he and Ruby had these at times—but for a writer just stepping onto the thin ice of actual character interaction, this was way too tricky. What was left was the classic situation of star-crossed lovers, a love forbidden by the strictures of two cultures or societies.

But none of these conflicts were meaningful anymore. To work, they had to be shocking, at least to the neighbors and immediate families. She was rich and he was poor? She could just give him half her money, or they could give it all away to charity. His family was snobbish high society and hers were ghetto and/or salt-of-the-earth? Ditto, who cared? Different religions? What if Nuri grew up and wanted to marry a little Christian or Jewish or Hindu girl from the other end of town?

The world population was so small now, as far as anyone knew, probably in grave danger of extinction, that he couldn't really imagine either set of parents objecting. A gay love story maybe? No, that wasn't very shocking anymore either, and he'd have no idea how to write it. All these things were old hat even *before* the Event, already the stuff of comedy.

And then it hit him. Love across species. Humans and aliens. Something *truly* star-crossed! Or maybe not even humans! Animals and aliens, maybe. It had probably been done before, though.

He paused a moment, getting a grip on himself. All those other writers were gone now, all the science fiction writers along with pretty much everybody else, as far as he could tell. He could relax and stop worrying about being derivative. As long as the story was new and fresh to *him*, it would be good enough. Because to create the literature of the post-Apocalypse, at least for now, there was only himself.

To revive the fast-becoming-lost art of literature, there was only Halycon Sage.

*I*t *was high time she contacted him*, thought Four. Her assignment from Commander Kennedy had been clear. But he was elusive. Having learned to move between Dry Creek Gulch and the Alternate Universe through Halycon Sage's cave, and possibly, by now, not even needing the cave but moving by his own powers alone, the cat was extremely elusive.

Ah. There he is.

He was truly a beautiful animal, she thought with admiration. His fur was like sunlight on honey, glistening and sweet-smelling, interspersed with white and darker orange in an intricate pattern. He moved with exquisite grace. His face was the essence of charm, with that requisite touch of humor. So beautifully designed, right down to the tiny dots from which the whiskers came.

There was a design like a scarab on his forehead. A "marmalade tabby," her research had informed her. *Well.* The humor: the white on his throat came up high onto his chin so that, at times, he looked as if he were wearing a neckerchief. At other moments he could look like an outraged rabbit.

She had been observing this subtle creature for a couple of weeks. He could open refrigerators, now pointless, but a good practice exercise. He could open cabinets, move rolling furniture, catch mice and chipmunks, and she was pretty sure he could read, although he had trouble turning the pages. He even spoke a few words of English, though his vocal cords were not suited for this at all.

He was loving to his human and animal friends, yet not sentimental. He knew how to control a situation. At times, though such a thing would seem impossible, she almost wished he were one of her own species.

Fatty Lumpkin stopped, observing the great being that stood before him. A great, shimmering creature, blue shading to purple, luminescent like the other Squid he had seen, but with something more. *How graceful she is*, he thought. *How well she moves. Almost as well as a cat.*

With such an odd and unexpected mutual attraction right from the beginning, it was no surprise that the diplomatic mission went well. By the time Four and Fatty Lumpkin had spoken briefly, the cat was firmly on her side, the side of the Squidren, the Sage-Preisczech Mind Meld, and the forces of good in general.

She had approached him very simply and honestly, and their discussion had been all business. Poor Lol-Bey. He had not seen what was immediately obvious to her: cats did not like poetry[5*].

---

5 Except possibly their own.

CHAPTER
THIRTY-SEVEN

Halycon Sage Has a Funny Turn

Voice: You know what a *funny* turn is, don't you? It's pronounced *funny* turn, not funny *turn*, and it's when you come over all funny.

Other Voice: (sarcastically) Well, *that's* helpful.

First Voice: Okay, well, it's when you *come over all queer*, then.

Second Voice: No, that's even worse. Here, let *me*. This is a British expression. It means you're minding your own business and suddenly you feel sick and a bit dizzy and faint and dejah-vooie, and just generally weird.

First Voice: As though *a goose was walking over your grave*! Oh, sorry, that's another one.

Second Voice: You just suddenly feel weird like that, as though you got caught in the crack between two timestreams, but then you shake yourself a bit and you're okay again.

Third Voice: (off camera) This is John Kennedy's fault. He's been studying British idioms.

This has been a public service message.

⌘

Halycon Sage really did feel weird for a minute though, as if he'd fallen down the gap between two chairs, but metaphysically. One moment he was sure everything was alright, that the world was tending in a good way, that people were working together to restore the Sacred Hoop, bring back the land and the animals, that humanity had passed a dangerous, dangerous crossroads and was on its way up. He breathed a tremendous sigh of relief.

That wasn't the funny turn—it was the place he started from.

Suddenly, the whole thing shifted into a kind of nightmare, like a negative photo of the first scenario. Everyone was fighting everyone else, split into little groups depending on who or where they were. This wasn't an argument-type fight; they were actually killing each other over this stuff. Most of the people were just incredibly frustrated and going crazy.

They were being asked to do stupid things that made no sense while being assured that *everything was fine right now*[26]. At the same time, a very small but incredibly powerful group of people were working hard every day to destroy everything: poison the rivers and oceans and kill the fish, chop down the forests so there was nothing left to make oxygen or hold the dirt to the ground, so that it slid into the water, stuff like that. Oh, and they were doing their best to start a nuclear war, too, which would obviously be the best way to destroy everything *really fast.*

Sage shook himself, coming out of it. That *couldn't* be the reality. It could not! But the weird thing was, he wasn't sure which one was real and which was his crazy imagination.

"See?" mumbled Sage to himself, alone in his cave. "You thought my book *Stranger* was a bunch of bull, didn't you? But listen to it! You don't understand yet that what I write is what's really going on."

> "Every time you think life can't get any stranger,
> it does. The strangeness is squared, cubed.
> What the heck?
> The End"

"*See?*"

Since Sage was still not sure which was the reality and which was the dream, or nightmare, he decided to just sit still for a while.

Maybe he really *was* a genius, as everyone had thought.

Attention.

Attention.

The following is brought to you by the LightSQUIDian Confederation, a new collaborative including followers of BOTH The Book of Lighted Squid and The Book of Squidly Light. You can see by the fact that we are working together that the situation is beyond desperate.

Are you listening, Halycon Sage? This is what you need to know.

Civilizations that have achieved time travel often believe any disaster can be walked back, that agents can travel back to before the disastrous timeline was initiated and change it. This is generally true.

The exception—are you listening, Halycon Sage? The exception is nuclear war. Nuclear war freezes the timeline and once initiated cannot be removed by any means known to Unvirtual Time Travel (UVTT), the Squidren of Squidship One, or any denizens of the known universe. Once it's done, it's done for good.

This has been a public service message.

—The LightSQUIDian Confederation,
est. 2019 C.E.[27]

After a while, the world steadied down a bit, and Halycon Sage began reflexively writing again. He wrote as he always did, putting down ideas and little bits as they struck him, then weaving them together later, a bit like making a braid from different-colored strands. But he could face neither his long novel nor anything else related to the Alternate Universe, the reality he had apparently created and which either was or was not a complete fiasco, and he had no idea which. He had started some story of no importance when he looked down and saw that the orange cat was back. Fatty Lumpkin, that was his name. He was making a funny noise and carrying something in his mouth.

Sage had apparently spent some time around bands as part of his mysterious past because he recognized the object right away as a black foam microphone cover. The peculiarity of the cat's vocalizations was the result of trying to talk while carrying this thing. The cat dropped it near Sage, then looked up at him beseechingly.

"What, you want to fetch?" asked Sage kindly.

Communication with this human was obviously impossible. The cat walked away.

Sage was tired from the crazy spinning of his universe and presently fell asleep. He dreamed he was looking at a sort of diary, and he knew somehow that it was a record of the cat's adventures, achievements, and frustrations. In the dream, this did not seem strange. He also knew that the cat was a *lawyer* (hence the atty. in his name), and this did not seem strange either, but quite natural. The book was open. He read the page before him and, when he woke, reproduced what was written there. Here is what it said:

12/30/16 Last night at about 2 a.m. (yes, alright, this morning), I delivered The Black Foam Ball of Ultimate Significance outside Father's door. (The humans absurdly refer to it as a microphone cover.) I announced its arrival with loud, impassioned cries emphasizing its urgency. (NOT with extreme yowling or funny noises. Honestly!) But once again, no action was taken, so I took it away again. They don't deserve it.

— F. Atty. Lumpkin, Esq.
(A Feline American)

Sage was a bit bemused when he awakened. *I wonder what that was about.* He looked around for the microphone cover in case it really was important, but it was gone.

He went back to calling the black dog.

"C'mon, pup, pup, pup. I know you've had it bad, but if you can just *get* here, we can make it better. You can be *my* dog. And you'll like No-Name Stupid. He likes dogs."

Sage was talking softly to the wall, trying to make his voice confident, comforting, and appealing, trying to be a dog whisperer. He was generally pretty good with animals.

"Come on, Sonar," he said, calling the dog by his name. "Good boy. Good doggie then."

CHAPTER
THIRTY-EIGHT

The Assembling of the Braided Thread

"**A** sword for the rat, a sword for the mole, a sword for the toad, a sword for the badger," quoted Basel Vasselschnauzer as he passed out various equipment to the new Braided Thread Teams. His heart was light, more than it had ever been in his life. He had friends, he had work, he was on the team, he was helping to save the Universe. This newfound happiness recalled *The Wind in the Willows*[28], one of the best animal stories ever written, and the brief period of his childhood before he became a cynic.

Actually, he was only passing out pens and paper, old fashioned note pads. These were a near-forgotten luxury in Dry Creek Gulch, but the Squid apparently had access to them. And since this meeting was on their ship, they were more than happy to supply anything Basel requested.

Griffin was announcing the teams. For the moment, he seemed to be in charge. Compared to many cultures, the Squid had few internal rivalries and power games. Though they had a firm hierarchy of seniority and respect with a code of manners like an intricate dance, they also tended to be practical, letting whoever *could* lead *do* it on any particular issue.

A roll call of those present from the four communities had yielded a surprising result. While the group contained many estimable constituents of the town, the Alternate Universe, the Squidship, and Unvirtual Time Travel, some notable personalities were missing. There was no Sage—no surprise there—no Ruby, no Jenny, no enigmatic cat, and no No-Name Stupid. Griffin, who didn't know the Dry Creek Gulchians, had no idea how strange this was.

It was decided to go ahead and assign those who were there.

"Red Thread: Spotted Snake. Abdurraheem. Emma. Nanobots." There was a faint sound as though a billion tiny noises made at the same time added up to something that sounded like mice giggling. The words "sandwiches" and "bubble baths" could be heard. Griffin sighed.

"Green Thread: All the eco-buffs from the Committees. Sophie, Trevor, Josh, you know who you are. Ape-Thing. Tarzun."

"Orangey-Yellow Thread," with a glance of apology at the Squidren for the slightly altered name. "Cat, Sparky, and Big D (because of the fire thing). Apocalypse Zombie. Time travelers."

"Blue Thread: Most of the Squidren. Miss O'Connell." (*Why her, I wonder,* thought Sophie.) "Basel Vasselschnauzer. Alexander Preisczech."

"Black Thread: Layla, Ratbone, zikr-going Squid, everybody else from the zikr. Preisczech, that gives you double duty. MysterySquid. Okay, who did I miss?"

There was a pause.

"Wait a minute," said Griffin suddenly, interrupting himself. "We've left out the most important person. Where's Halycon Sage? We can't do it without him. He's *pivotal.*"

"Maybe you should answer his letter," suggested Muhammad Wang Smith. "He's probably been waiting to hear from you."

"Good idea," said Griffin. He pulled a pen and paper out of his pocket and began to write. Those nearest him craned forward with interest, wondering what he would say.

Dear Halycon Sage,

I am in receipt of ~~your letter dated~~ your letter emerging from somewhere within the space-time continuum. It is always good to hear from my readers.

Thank you for your concerns about the dog. I was not that happy with the situation myself and have decided to accede to your request. The dog will be coming for you shortly.

Please accompany him to the Squidship without delay. There is work to be done, Halycon Sage.

The game's afoot, Watson!

Yours Sincerely,

Rupert Griffin

Griffin felt good quoting Sherlock Homes in a letter to Halycon Sage. Sage's novels (and some of his thoughts, which were leaking though the space-time continuum) showed him to be quite familiar with British idioms.

"What will you do with it?" asked Preisczech with some interest.

"Put it through the wall, of course," said Griffin. "Where do you access?" He turned to the Squids.

"Right over here," said Obiwan Mohammed, indicating something that looked like a mail slot in the wall of the ship.

Griffin folded his letter neatly in thirds and inserted it into the slot. It was gone.

Something else happened on the ship that was of no great cosmic significance but was quite important to *one* person, anyway. Inexplicably, the Apocalypse Zombie had shown up and joined the rest of the merry gathering aboard ship. Nobody had questioned his right to be there, but Obiwan Mohammed and Muhammad Wang Smith had been staring at him for several minutes, talking in an undertone. The Zombie found this insulting and was considering *doing* something about it. Before he could, Muhammad Wang Smith stepped up to him and touched him gently on the arm with a long, soft tentacle.

"Tell me, sir, your *face* . . ."

"What about it?" asked Edgar sullenly. "I'm a zombie, what do you want?"

"Oh?" she parried. "I've heard that you were an artist and former college student." The Squid had almost endless sources of information. The Zombie's jaw dropped, at least as far as it would go. "I was wondering if perhaps you thought you had leprosy."

Now Edgar was truly stunned. *Of course* he had leprosy. This was the explanation for all his odd behavior, as well as his newly assumed identity.

"Because . . . " She made a sort of Japanese fan of her tentacle tip and hid her smile behind it coyly (some of these Squidresses were feminine beyond belief, and it did need to be seen to be believed), "because I think, sir, that you should read *'The Adventure of the Blanched Soldier '* by Sir Arthur Conan Doyle[29].

"Based on the information provided therein by a fictional but eminent London specialist, Dr. James Saunders, we believe you have ichthyosis, or pseudo-leprosy."

"A disease that is quite treatable," they said together. And they turned away, leaving him to contemplate the possibility of a new life.

✑

There was one more thing to be done, and Commander Kennedy had been dreading it, but there was no getting out of it now. The Braided Thread Teams were organized and on the point of deploying to their various assignments.

For all this time, the Squidiler had kept the zi out of sight, giving them on-ship research projects or letting them party in the Squidpool, afraid that their strangeness would alienate the otherwise accommodating Earth culture. They were just too different. But now there was no getting around it. The zi were needed on the Teams, both for their vast expertise and talent and for their sheer numbers—the Eartheans would just have to deal with it.

"Excuse me, one moment." He used his most official voice, commanding instant respect and attention from the excited crowd of Squidren and volunteers.

"People and creatures of Earth, the galaxies, and the Alternate Universe. There are some other members of our crew that you must meet. They are necessary to this mission, and your meeting them can no longer be put off. This is a warning: they will appear strange and different to you, but I beg you to rise above your cultural prejudices and accept them. Let me repeat, *we need them.*"

There. If that wouldn't do it, nothing would.

On cue, a thin, translucent panel slid back, revealing the large area containing the Squidpool and various other facilities. In this wide doorway stood the rest of the Squidren, the zi-chen, about thirty of them. They were magnificent! Tall and shimmering, their deep blue bodies shading to magenta, not to green (male Squidren) or purple (female)[30], as the Earthers had seen before.

The Earthers broke out in spontaneous applause. Kennedy and his cohort stared at them in total incomprehension. The Earthers stared back, equally baffled.

Ratbone reached to fill the silence. "So, these are the zi we've been hearing so much about? Pleased to meet you, zizes and zentlemen. You're lookin' *fine* tonight!"

"But," Four, now senior diplomat of the Squidren, felt compelled to engage, "aren't you shocked? Don't you have a kind of sick feeling in your stomach?"

Sophie was outraged. "*What?* Because of their *gender?* That's nothing! One of my cousins is gay, and my eighth grade homeroom teacher was transgender. So are lots of people! Is *that* why you've been keeping them hidden all this time?"

Four was equally bemused. "*Gender?* What do you mean?" She looked at the commander helplessly. Her eyes met the eyes of John Chang, and for once the two were in accord. This was about the weirdest thing that had happened yet.

Chang came bravely to her rescue, stating the issue bluntly. He turned toward the Earthers. Whatever their reaction, even if it included violence, he was prepared to accept it.

"Can't you *see*?" asked John Chang in a gentle voice. His audience was breathless. "Don't you have *eyes?* They're *magenta*!"

The room exploded in laughter. The Dry Gulchers, Alternate Universers, Spotted Snake, Ape-Thing, Griffin, and everybody else who was not a Squid laughed for fully five minutes. After the zi-chen stepped out into the welcoming crowd, it took the Earthers a long time to explain to the Squid exactly what was so funny.

A little while later, when things had calmed down, Commander Kennedy checked in with Rupert Griffin.

"Have you heard anything from Sage yet?"

"No, I thought *you'd* tell *me*. Isn't there anything in the mail slot?"

"Nothing. TechieSquid has been checking every quarter hour. It's completely empty."

"This is odd. I wrote a whole new chapter of *Novel*, a revised edition. Yes, I went that far! I saved the dog, Sonar, and sent him to the Time-Space cave with explicit instructions to *fetch Halycon Sage*."

"Well, I'm sure *I* don't know," said Kennedy, suddenly reverting to his modest and slightly uncertain pre-commander personality. "Why don't you go off somewhere and write a prologue or something? Give it another shot of adrenalin."

Wondering how a Squid would know about adrenalin, Griffin went away to comply with this sensible suggestion.

Suddenly, there was a new disturbance: Ruby came bursting in, improbably riding No-Name Stupid. In fact, they came at a gallop through the side of the Squidship, which, being imaginary anyway, was easily penetrable by those who knew how.

Ruby knew exactly who and what she wanted, and she wasted no time in claiming it. After quickly ascertaining that the actual object of her quest was not among the company, she spoke, and was instantly obeyed.

"Come on, Katzenpauzer, let's blow this pop stand. It's time to find Halycon Sage again."

*I*t *feels so familiar*, thought Ruby, *heading out on No-Name Stupid to find Halycon Sage*. History did indeed repeat itself, not always of course, but sometimes, and it was certainly doing so now. The clopping sound of the horse's hooves on the paved road, then the gentler sound of hooves on dry, packed dirt. The peaceful jogging of their motion. Ruby had decided a trot was more appropriate than a gallop at this point, though that could change. Like Sage, she could ride easily without saddle or bridle, holding the silky mane but giving commands with sounds and the pressure of her knees. She did so now.

Stupid was pleased with the adventure. It was good to be a brown and white pinto on a mission again, though he had grown tired of it during the seemingly endless alternation of motels and campfires while Sage had been trying to save the world. As before, though Sage was a good rider and a kind friend, Stupid was glad to be with Ruby, the horse whisperer. He never had to explain anything to her. Perhaps, in her case, he was a human whisperer.

Though she was not yet instituting a gallop, Ruby had grown more concerned about Halycon Sage. Going off on some artistic quest or monk-like retreat was quite typical of him, and neither of them was overly dependent on the other, but this had become ridiculous.

Her conscience was bothering her a little too, although mostly she just missed him. What if he had broken a leg falling into some canyon or gone so far into that cave he frequented that he had gotten lost? The picture of him starving alone somewhere while she'd been thinking *He'll come back when he's ready* was quite distressing. She nudged Stupid gently with her heels, moving them into a canter.

Her first idea was to try the cave, and she reached it after about an hour. It would not have been so useful for food storage if it had been farther away. She dismounted and entered the cave mouth, Stupid walking behind her. It was wide and tall at this point. She didn't know how high the cave ceiling was further down, past the community area, but she could always tell him to wait for her.

"Sage! Halycon *Sage!*" No response, hardly even an echo. They walked further, calling at intervals, looking down the various chambers that opened up. It was a really big cave system, bigger than she'd remembered. They walked down any path that seemed promising.

"Halycon Sage, come out of there! Enough of this crap, it's time to come home!"

Nothing.

Ruby had her pride, but that was nothing now.

"Sage, if it's something I did, I'm *sorry!*"

Sorry, sorry, sorry, sorry, replied the cave. They'd reached a place where there was an echo. Nothing else, though.

She threw it all to the winds.

"Sage, *I love you!*" Not that she hadn't said this before, but she'd never shouted it out at the top of her lungs.

"HALYCON SAGE, ALRIGHT, *I WILL MARRY YOU!* DO YOU HEAR ME? WE CAN HAVE RATBONE DO IT, OR LAYLA."

There was nothing, nothing, nothing. She was almost crying, and Stupid had moved away a little because her voice was so loud.

Suddenly, Stupid bounced back from thin air (again!) in a way that would have been comic in less dire circumstances. He lost his balance, stumbling, almost falling, a pretty neat trick for a creature with four legs.

Ordinarily, he would have been all offended dignity, but that was the furthest thing from his mind now.

Both Stupid and Ruby grasped the situation instantly. Somebody, or something, did not want anyone to find Halycon Sage.

CHAPTER

THIRTY-NINE

In the midst of the many dreams and visions which alternated between the ecstatic and the terrifying, Halycon Sage had one extremely silly one. Older residents of Dry Gulch Creek and the Alternate Universe may remember, in the early days of the internet, an absurd, fruity kind of voice announcing, with moronic enthusiasm, "You've got *mail!*"

Halycon Sage had never been a fan of the internet, using it only reluctantly at the town library to send manuscripts to his editor, but he remembered this phrase and this voice. His dream offered him a variation. "You've got *SQUID!*" the dream voice enthused.

There was nothing more, just this absurd message. Sage emphatically did *not* have Squid. He did not have *anybody*. Right now, with no Ruby, no dog, no cat, and no No-Name Stupid, he would have been exceedingly *glad* to see a Squid. He thought he heard barking, too, the sharp, urgent bark of a large dog, but it turned out to be nothing.

The universe swung sickeningly, like a midway ride out of control. Sage was getting used to it, but it was still pretty unpleasant. In and out of alignment it swung, forming one pattern, then the other. Sage must have done a bit of drinking at some point because this somehow reminded him of the worst aspects of overuse combined with a king-sized hangover. Or maybe it reminded him of the time he'd been beaten and robbed in an alley, the incident that had caused his amnesia and incidentally led to his new career and his worldwide fame. Not that it mattered either way.

It seemed as though something new was happening. The shadowy stick figure had been appearing more frequently, but Sage couldn't quite catch it with his eye. It was a thing of corners and interstices. Beyond that, and who knew what the connection was or if there even was one, the situation in the nightmare iteration of the Alternate Reality seemed to be growing worse.

The Universe held its breath.
There was a soundless explosion.
Too loud for sound, too far away, but also near.
Not far away from anywhere.

Dear God. Dear God.

One of the dictators had Pushed the Button.

And all the others were responding.

There was one more interaction in Halycon Sage's cave before the end. First, he had just a few moments to notice things: that he was quite calm, that he still loved Ruby, and that his only regrets besides not seeing her again were that Griffin had not answered his letter and he had never met the dog.

The stick figure, hitherto known as Stetson Black and the Shadowy Man, stepped out of the corner. If you have read the first Chronicle, you might have suspected that he was someone we have met before, the nihilist author of novels including *The Black Gray Dark*, *Decay*, and *The Swamp of Despair* and the nonfiction works *Filling the Void with Talk Shows* and *I'm Fabulous, You're a Necrotic Collection of Worm-Food*. The one who almost destroyed the world the *last* time only to be foiled by No-Name Stupid. There was a timeless pause while the two men looked at each other.

"*I hate you, Halycon Sage,*" said Niemand Kompt, focusing all the malevolent force of his being down to this one scalding phrase.

"And I love you *too*," replied Halycon Sage with a little smile, slightly ironic, but not unkind.

Once again, Niemand Kompt had been outclassed, left miles behind. He would *never* be Halycon Sage's nemesis. For Sage had not even spoken his name.

And then everything was over.

CHAPTER
FORTY

Suddenly, everyone was in the cave at once. The first arrival announced himself with a loud volley of barking. Finally, after Griffin's focused writings and urgent commands to "Fetch!" and Sage's concentrated repetitions of, "Here, Sonar, c'mon boy," and similar things, the big black Labrador retriever had made it through. He exploded out of the wall and launched himself at Sage, licking his face in an ecstasy of affection.

Next, Tarzun came swinging in from nowhere on ropes made of nothing, yelling his perfect yell. A few moments later, Lol-Bey slithered in from the cave mouth. He apparently had the skills, either technical or natural, to penetrate the barrier, and he had done his research before arriving.

"You! They call you the Shadowy Man! You're that crazy writer, Niemand Kompt. You want to destroy the world." Lol-Bey was now an expert on Earth culture.

Kompt bowed ceremoniously.

"I will fight you!" declared the Squid and prepared to do so, but a series of new arrivals got in his way.

Next up, Ruby and Stupid came through the wall at a gallop, followed closely by Basel Vasselschnauzer on a small unicycle. (Don't ask.) In only a moment, he had seen and identified the two authors.

"Mr. Sage," said Basel, tipping his hat. "And *you*," he turned to the other, dripping contempt. "Your work is thin and derivative. You are not fit to be a bus boy at the Algonquin, and when the world rights itself and I return to my column, I shall squash you like a bug."

"But the world will *not* right itself," said Niemand Kompt. For once he had a point.

We will draw an editorial veil over the meeting of Ruby and Halycon Sage after so long apart. Suffice it to say, they were very glad to see each other.

The Orange Thread Team was there, but they were reduced to chaos by the apparent hysteria of their feline leader who was running around in circles emitting the most piteous meows.

Four, as adept at languages as she was at diplomacy, translated.

"Where is it? Have you lost it, you fools? Why didn't you listen to me? We need it! We need it NOW!"

Nobody could make anything of this without translation; with it, they realized that what they had taken for the senseless wailings of the classic cat-noise were in truth frantic appeals for haste. "Now, now, NOW!"

The Black Thread Team—Layla, Ratbone, Preisczech, and four Squid—lit a candle in one corner, made a circle around it, and began chanting rhythmic and powerful prayers. It should have seemed ridiculous, but for some reason, it did not. Nuri would normally have been with them, but he was trying to pull away.

"What is it, habibi?" asked his mother, bending down.

"We need my friend! We need my friend!" cried Nuri.

"But all your friends are *here!*" She indicated Ratbone, Sage, Ruby, Stupid, and the Braided Thread Teams. "Almost everyone is here."

"Not the one we need!" sobbed Nuri. He was conscious of humiliation. Now that he had finally turned four, he should not be acting like this. But without his friend from across the stars, they could do nothing. Apparently he and the cat were of one mind: that something *great* was needed, something beyond the ordinary wonders of space-time movement, psychic ability, earthly genius, and alien technology.

Without that extra something—or *two* somethings unless Nuri's friend and whatever the cat was looking for turned out to be the same thing—the nuclear destruction of the world now occurring could not be reversed. Don't ask how they knew this. They just did. And they were right.

"Are these what you're looking for?" asked Jenny politely, suddenly appearing out of thin air. She was just as soft looking and beautiful as ever, with her light brown, silky feathered hair, chocolate colored eyes, and pretty mouth. The hard work had only chapped her hands, and she had acquired a few laughter lines from being with Preisczech and a few worry lines from the previous End of the World, hitherto known as the Event.

But she was Jenny and not Jenny, as though she had partially thrown off a congenial but somewhat limiting disguise. Her image shimmered from one being to the other, and the Jenny they knew was certainly *one* of them.

"Empress!" cried the Squidren, sinking as one into a deep bow. Not all of them had seen her before, but all of them knew.

"Well, my friend, you certainly get around," remarked Ruby, swallowing a couple of times and adjusting to the new situation.

The newly revealed Head Honcha of a pretty significant portion of the universe turned briefly to Preisczech.

"I'm sorry, love, I tried to tell you; there just never seemed to be a good time. But I've searched for you through a hundred thousand galaxies, and I'm still your Jenny if you want me."

Preisczech's on-again off-again English wobbled a little, but he replied with quiet dignity. "Is okay with me, Jenny, you are number one A-Okay with me. I *knew* you have secret."

"Someone else is doing it too," remarked Nuri, suddenly calm. He was looking in the other direction, and everyone followed his gaze. There was Four, and then Miss O'Connell, then Four, then Miss O'Connell, blinking back and forth like a neon sign.

"I told you I was working under cover," Four remarked a bit apologetically. And she shifted once again.

"MysterySquid!" shouted TechieSquid and Lol-Bey. Only they had spent enough time around MysterySquid to be sure. MysterySquid, whose satin black was without any phosphorescence and who never showed the second color of the other Squid, who would be here and gone and here again with no one noticing, who said nothing, ever, but only watched and listened.

"Miss O'Connell!" exclaimed Rupert Griffin, clearly surprised to find that UVTT's efficient secretary—the one who typed perfect papers, ran communications, and provided Veggie-Bugs to the Ape-Thing, water to the Spotted Snake, and hot tea and coffee to everyone else—was a Squid. He, too, swallowed a couple of times.

"MysterySquid?" asked Lol-Bey again. He did not have the nerve to address the Empress. "Were you the ones who put a Barrier over this part of the cave?"

"We had to," she said apologetically, shifting to Miss O'Connell. "We had to see if Halycon Sage could write us all out of this mess. And perhaps he has."

CHAPTER

FORTY-ONE

upert Griffin cleared his throat. "I wonder if all you lovebirds and shapeshifters could put a hold on it till we save the world. This whole nuclear war thing is a fairly high priority."

Jenny blushed, a charming thing to see on a seven-foot imperial blue Squid Empress who was simultaneously a wonderful young woman from Earth. Ceremoniously, she held out her hands.

The left hand moved toward F. Atty. Lumpkin, Esq., a.k.a. Fatty Lumpkin, Feline American and Orange Cat of Earth.

With the right hand, she reached out to Nuri Muhammad Wadood ibn-Abdurraheem Hussain, recently turned four. In one hand was the Black Foam Ball of Ultimate Significance. In the other was the Cuttlefish.

For a few moments, everyone was silent. Somehow, now when there was no time to waste, there was all the time in the world. Some knew almost all of what was happening, and some knew almost nothing.

The Squidren knew, and we have doubtless laughed at them for this, that small children of whatever species are the most powerful beings in the universe.

Nuri knew that nothing could save the world except his friend the Cuttlefish, though he did not know why.

F. Atty Lumpkin knew that the Black Foam Ball of Ultimate Significance held the key to everything. He knew something about what it was and how it worked, though not everything.

A number of those assembled, including Sage, Ratbone, Layla, and assorted Squid, knew positively that God existed. An approximately equal number were pretty sure that He (She? Zi?) did not.

Niemand Kompt knew that he did not love or trust or even like any single, solitary being in any universe, in the whole multiverse, and that he would take all existence down with him if he could.

The Squidren knew the Empress could do anything.

A number of the creatures there, within and across different species, knew that they had learned to trust each other. And everybody present knew that nuclear war would destroy the world of Dry Creek Gulch, the Mirror World of the Alternate Reality, and, by means of a chain reaction, very likely both their wider universes.

So, with everything riding on one throw of the dice, with everyone waiting in silence, there was a little space, the strange kind of peace and quiet that comes when nothing is left to be done.

We can make this simple, or we can make it complicated with a lot of running around. Let's make it simple.

Jenny looked at Nuri and the cat. "Do you know what to do with them?"

Nuri nodded, and the cat gave a mysterious cat-smile by inclining his head to the right so that he *appeared* to be smiling (since cats can't actually smile). His peridot eyes were as intense as Four had ever seen them.

The circle was wide, and everyone could see what happened next. Jenny stepped back. Nuri cradled the Cuttlefish in his two hands and held zi toward the Black Foam Ball of Ultimate Significance. The cat had managed to turn the ball in his mouth. Now the opening, where anyone foolish enough to consider it a microphone cover would have inserted the mike, was facing toward the boy. Nuri held the Cuttlefish closer to the hole. The Cuttlefish crawled into the hole and disappeared. And so did everything else.

There was nothing. Not the nothing of nuclear destruction or the nothing of Niemand Kompt's poisonous nihilism, but a nothing that was infinite clear light, consciousness without an object.

It was utterly real and aware.

No emotion or intelligence were perceptible, but that was because this was the *origin* of emotion and intelligence. It preceded them. There was no time, no space, no near and far, no worry, no sadness, and no joy in any usual sense. Yet each individual locus of consciousness was there, each being, now unaware of their bodies, their cultures, and mostly unaware of their personalities. Yet some indefinable kernel of individuality remained. They were not separate from the infinite clear awareness of light that was more than light.

For a timeless time, nothing happened.

There was a sense of this highest energy stepping down just a little, growing infinitesimally nearer to what beings consider manifestation, the place of actions and objects. A sort of golden mist arose, faintly tinged with a light intoxication of ecstasy.

Now there was bliss, *now* there were joy and love.

Every being who had been in the cave was included, and many more besides. None were left out.

At some point, the energy moved again. An intention appeared, not in words, but everyone understood. It had a certain graciousness, and all the time in the world.

"Do you have questions?"

From a Squid: Why are little children the most powerful beings of all?

Answer: Because they remember.

From Halycon Sage: Is it really all worthwhile?

Answer: Yes.

Unidentified Citizen: Why does the name of our town keep changing?

Answer: Reality is in flux. There are always these little variations, often unnoticed.

From Niemand Kompt: Does anybody love me?

Answer: Yes.

Commander John Kennedy and Rupert Griffin pulled themselves together enough to glance at each other. That was not easy in this atmosphere; in fact, it was almost impossible. One nodded to the other, and the other one spoke their mutual question.

Squid/Griffin: How will this that's happening here and now save the multiverse?

(They had no doubt it would—that much was obvious. But a small part of each of them retained the memory of leadership, that this was their responsibility.)

Answer: Oh. (There was almost a laugh. And how interesting to find that humor lay so close to the heart of things.) The moving of the Cuttlefish Friend into the Black Foam Ball of Ultimate Significance breaks the lock on space-time caused by the nuclear war. You can go back now, to before it happened. You get a do-over.

Slowly the scene faded, and the beings in the cave drifted gently back to their individual bodies and personalities. But these were unspeakably altered. Everyone was silent, still, at peace.

The only sound was Niemand Kompt, sobbing and sobbing as if his heart would break.

After a few moments, Halycon Sage stepped over and gave him a hug.

CHAPTER
FORTY-TWO

Before the apotheosis of everyone in the cave, the Blue Thread Team, assigned to the Mad Grammarians and small children of the Alternate Universe, had been momentarily stymied by the onset of nuclear war, which rendered their plans useless.

As they slowly returned to Earth consciousness they realized that Jenny's intervention and the subsequent happenings would allow them to go back in time. They had to gauge it just right: maybe two precious weeks before the war.

The Team took a deep breath and stormed through the wall into the Home for Delusional Grammarians, already friends of the Squidren. The cat came too. Preisczech and Vasselschnauzer and the rest of the Blue Thread Team started the revolution right there, as a good revolution *should* be started: with powerful words.

The dam was well and truly broken, and Squid came pouring through, not only those from the Squidship, but others from around the multiverse who had been called in. (Why the Squid at some points use conventional travel and at others merely teleport remains a mystery to our scientists. —Sophie MacGregor et al.) The portal between Halycon Sage's cave and the Home for Delusional Grammarians was fully established, a wide open Chunnel of time and space.

Old Pete was slumped in a wheelchair in front of the television. He kept hoping that Jeopardy would come on, but since it hadn't been showing on any TV he could access since 1979, he spent a lot of time dozing.

Agnes sat beside him. She wore a flower-print housedress that snapped down the front. She had once been Ms. Carlotta Echevaria (a very distant cousin of Ruby's) and had dressed in smart black and white fashions, heels clicking crisply down the echoing halls of learning. But now she had adopted a name and costume more appropriate to her new role, for she had taught theatre as well as English. Agnes had found that if she sat in just the right spot in front of the television, she could see interesting pictures in her mind.

Old Pete and Agnes were only two representatives of the vast class of institutionalized Delusional Grammarians. There were thousands more like them: dedicated, eccentric, in love with words, now shambling like zombies, full of depressants and anti-depressants.

But suddenly the Squid came pouring through, and everything changed. Soon, history would record the

Slither on Washington, one hundred thousand thousand Squid, too many to count, swimming through time and space to every part of the country and converging on the nation's capital, accompanied by one million Delusional Grammarians—delusional no more!—marching, chanting, and waving signs.

"Fewer Not Less!" the signs proclaimed. And "Lay and Lie: Get it right!"

And indeed, the dictator was a *liar*, and one who *lay* in the Presidential Bed where he did not belong. And the Squid, the Mad Grammarians, the Small Children, and the people of the country took him down.

About a week later, Halycon Sage happened on two friends as he was walking up a tree-lined street in Dry Creek Gulch one sunny morning: Fatty Lumpkin and the Squidress Four.

"Here's your wedding present," said Halycon Sage, handing them a scroll. It was tied with deep blue ribbon, and he had decorated it himself. It was not very long, but of all the things he had ever written, it was the one he liked the best.

Romance for Cat and Squid
by Halycon Sage

He had assumed a human form. He stood there tall and slim, courtly and rebellious, lithe

303

and urbane and dangerous. The setting sun on his red-gold hair made a second sun below.

"Did you think I was really a cat?" he asked her softly.

"Is anyone really a cat?" she parried lightly, weaving a blue tentacle behind her in a gesture of indescribable grace.

He thought a moment, then threw caution to the winds.

"*Everyone* is a cat," he replied.

The End

The two parties were pleased but somewhat embarrassed. Though their mutual affection and admiration were real, Four had begun liking John Chang a bit better in light of recent events, and Fatty Lumpkin felt inclined to keep his options open. As usual, Halycon Sage could not tell the difference between the stuff that really happened and the stuff he made up.

CHAPTER
FORTY-THREE

The Five-Stranded Braid

his is a braid of five strands: The Red, the Green, the Yellow, the Blue, and the Black. One by one, they step on stage. One by one, they are introduced. The braids, ever each the same, are modified by time and place. Here are the braids of Earth, for a time beyond imagining, a time long yet to come.

The Red: In this case, Red and Silver. Close enough. When the structure of evil is demolished, only half the work is done. Only a third of the work. The web must be rebuilt, this time for everyone. That is the second third. Finally, the Insensate must Awaken, the Unconscious become Conscious. All Hail the Red and Silver.

The Green: The Land must be protected, and here the land is Green (or much of it). The Land, Sky, Water, Air, Mountains, Plants, Creatures must be protected and nourished. The plants and creatures must be revived, blessed, comforted, and loved. All Hail the Green.

The Yellow: The Eartheans have a color they call orange. Close enough. The leader of the Yellow is a quadruped, decorated with alternating bands of light and dark, luminous-eyed, brilliant, but without speech. The Yellow is Light and Fire, Cleverness and Wisdom, more. All Hail the Yellow.

The Blue: Visitors come, the Blue Ones. They save, they guard, they heal. Without them, impetuous Earth would destroy itself; its dominant species would destroy everything. Power and Gentleness of Water. Cetaceans join them. All Hail the Blue.

The Black: Everything that is left, everything that is mysterious and unrevealed. The Brilliant Darkness of True Religion, equal to its Light. The color of the Eartheans (though some have grown paler through contrasting climates). The Color of the Catalyst: Halycon Sage. All Hail the Black!

"For The Book of Squidly Light *was always appropriate to the person who was reading it.*
Whatever was needed was what it said."
—Unknown Author

—The Book of Squidly Light

Halycon Sage stared. His quirky writer's mind was always shifting between worlds and dimensions, reality and fantasy, tragedy and laughter. Surely this was one such instance. He shut his eyes, breathed, looked again. It was still there. "The Catalyst: Halycon Sage."

A postscript, in odd, wavery handwriting appeared below.

"Don't be so surprised, Halycon Sage. If a cat can be the Yellow Thread, surely you can be part of the Black Thread. Besides, two others here are part of it also. So don't indulge in false modesty. Get over yourself."

The Squid were evidently picking up a bit of human idiom. Sage thought instantly of Layla and Ratbone as the probable candidates and decided to try out their zikr.

On the final page was written, "A Word from the Wise Eartheans." Halycon Sage looked to see what it said.

O distant, ancient thinker,
who wrote, "all is water,"
fluid, cool, transparent, deep,
sometimes I feel that all is light;
and as you were surely asked:
how are trees and stones of water?
so they will ask me:
what of mud and sorrow?
You may have argued,
but records of your words do not survive
and so, writing for a thousand years from now,
I simply assert
that all is light:
the sea, the hills, the horses, the symphonies . . .

not sunlight, mind you,
crude, natural cousin to what I mean . . .
but enough of this,
for I might say more than
all I want
inscribed on the dancing flames of my pyre:
the enigmatic phrase,
all is light;
and may time be as kind to me as you,
ancient brother,
and may my words,
preserved by miraculous accident,
find a kindred spirit.[31]

"Huh," said Halycon Sage, his thinking noise. *What of mud and sorrow?* caught his eye. Mud—all the gross, ugly, disgusting stuff he couldn't stand, things you read or saw or someone said, things that left a dirty track in the mind making you wish your brain could throw up, and a momentary fear that it could never be washed clean. Sorrow—the hunger, the torture, the loneliness, the suffering of animals and children, the senseless cutting of sacred trees, the things that, all his life, he could never stand, never bear, never accept.

The mystical and light-filled earthor (*Earth author = earthor*; Sage's game-playing mind was irrepressible even at such a moment) . . . the earthor did not explain what of mud and sorrow. In his younger days, Sage would have styled this a copout.

Not now.

Now he knew that some things had to be experienced first-hand, and that other things could never be put into words.

The End

EPILOGUE

A good way upstream in the ascending levels of vibration, a conversation was going on. "I'm a bit puzzled," said the Adequately Magnificent Presence to one of the Equerries. "These Squid use five colored strands in their Braided Thread schematic of reality, yet most cultures throughout the Multiverse use seven, eight, nine, eleven, or some multiple thereof. It is generally believed that those are the superior numbers. *Five . . .*" zi shook zi's heads.

"Are they unaware of the Purple, the Violet, or the other colors? Their neglect of Magenta, in itself, is shocking," hazarded the first Equerry.

"The Squid are wise in many ways, but their knowledge is incomplete," confirmed the Second Equerry. "It is possible that they have conflated two or more colors or done something else anomalous but not ultimately invalidating."

"Well, then," said the Presence, preparing to lean back/dissolve/relax for a few hundred millennia, "We shall wait and see."

AFTERWORD

Deepest gratitude to Sheila Hixon, Jinen Angyo Sensei, for permission to use her husband's poem asserting that "all is light" with which the main story closes. It was written in his youth and has not been previously published.

Lex Hixon (Shaykh Nur al-Jerrahi) was the great teacher of my life, considered by many to be enlightened. The apotheosis experienced by my characters in Chapter 41 owes a debt to his initiatic vision described in Chapter Five of *Coming Home: The Experience of Enlightenment in Sacred Traditions*.

Like the metaphysical system of the Squidren, *The Book of Squidly Light* contains various threads:

- life in a post-apocalyptic desert town
- multicultural people and cross-cultural or cross-species romances
- the thoughts and behaviours of space aliens
- suddenly-sentient nanobots
- rituals—both holy and unholy
- poetry written by cats and horses

- a critique of some life-denying attitudes that threaten us all
- and even a few Secrets of the Universe

One important thread deals with the time-traveling exploits of characters including a Shadowy Man, the dimension-hopping Squidren, and author Rupert Griffin. While Griffin, his book *Novel*, and the dog Sonar are imaginary, Robert Grudin and his novel *Book* are real.

The tragic fate of *Book's* dog Doppler inspired me to write to Professor Grudin requesting an alternate ending. I never wrote that letter, but Halycon Sage did, bringing justice and love to one imaginary dog.

May justice, love, wisdom, and healing likewise come to animals, humans, ecosystems, galaxies, dimensions, and to all beings.

Amin.[6]

---

6 To read more intriguing and funny stuff you won't find in the book, please join us at our Author site: https:// karimavargsbushnell.com

ACKNOWLEDGEMENTS

Having written this whole kitten caboodle—I *like* spelling it that way, I have *cats*—it only remains to thank those who got me here. You are old friends, new friends, friends who are family and family who are friends, and I can't thank you enough.

Jeneane Harter, producer and outsource wrangler extraordinaire.

Beta Readers Elizabeth Bushnell, Faye Howell, and John Hakim Bushnell.

Editors Rabbi Yonassan Gershom, B.C. Hatch, and Chandi Lyn.

Artists Faye Howell, (No-Name Stupid and bar sign), B.C. Hatch and Pankaj Runthala (Layout and interior design), and Richard Ljoenes (Cover).

Garek Bushnell, unfailing support and voice of the *Halycon Sage* trailer video at the author website, https://karimavargasbushnell.com, and Aziza Kay Grace, simply for being there.

Bob, a Comfort Cat, large of body and spirit, "not lost but gone before," and Ginger from Egypt (*Zanjabil min-Misr*), the new Red Cat on duty.

To all of you: this writer has no adjectives glorious enough to sing your praises. If *The Book of Squidly Light* reaches people in a powerful way, part of the credit is yours.

Ongoing thanks to my mother for a gift that can never be repaid: she trained me in words as others are trained in sports.

Deep gratitude to my current teachers, Shaykha Fariha Fatima al-Jerrahi and Imam Bilal Hyde for their ceaseless efforts, diametrically opposed types of wisdom and knowledge, and boundless generosity toward this humble student.

Final Note: the cat Fatty Lumpkin (F. Atty. Lumpkin, esq.) was pretty much as described, though he may or may not have numbered reading and time travel among his accomplishments. His adventures and exploits are chronicled in *Sage's Multi-Verse Mini-Series.*

APPENDIX A

From the Editor: This might be a good time to answer a question that has baffled readers of The Sage Chronicles since the publication of the first book, now called *The Way Beyond* formerly called *The Life and Times of Halycon Sage* since its publication—well, has baffled two or three of them, anyway.

What on earth led to Halycon Sage becoming Ruby's favorite author?

Ruby has been described as, and has shown herself by her actions to be, intelligent—also, a woman of few words. Why would such a person be interested in the minimalist two-sentence drivel, the obscurity, art-for-annoyance's-sake (as some would have it), or even in the longer attenuated babblings of Halycon Sage? And yes, this is the view of him held by his detractors. But even viewing his novels in the most positive light—terse, Zen-like works of focused genius—how could she have spent all those stolen hours away from the Dirty Dog Gang in reading and re-reading them? After all, you can read the entire corpus of his work in about five minutes.

So? You ask.

Yes? We reply.

You said you were going to tell us, you pursue.

Oh, we respond, sheepishly brushing our hair off our forehead with a nervous gesture. Well. The Zen allusion is not altogether off the mark. Ruby finds the works of Halycon Sage meditative. Some writings are all surface, naked to discovery at first reading, and readers in the global West *expect* them to be this way. But in some strange manner, Sage's work and way of thinking are more like the products of the global East, clues to a depth that needs to be mined, unveiled over time. This is easier to understand since the advent of the internet and the interesting concept of the zip file. (Some of us can never get them to *un*zip, but that is beyond the scope of this discussion.)

It has been suggested, to cite one example, that the Qur'an[32] in Arabic works this way: not as a straightforward text proceeding from start to finish, but as something loose in time and space, an interactive experience where different occurrences of the same word are related and shades of meaning transfer from one occurrence to another. The text adjusts itself, sometimes rejecting the reader as completely as a slammed door, at other times opening out into surprising insights. In its own infinitely smaller way, the work of Halycon Sage acts in a similar manner.

To understand how deeper implications and complexities can be unwrapped from even Sage's simplest writings, it is only necessary to examine his novel *Man*

Reading a Book. In *The Way Beyond*, we read this opus and its interpretation:

'There was a man reading a book and it said there was a man reading a book and it said there was a man reading a book and it said there was a man reading a book and it said . . .'

Like all of his books, this one made a deeper point than was apparent on the surface. If no one does or creates anything original, if everyone merely reposts the sayings of others and lives vicariously through second-hand experience, eventually the only thing to read about or view will be someone reading about or viewing something. Whether anyone would get this subtle point was another matter.

He had no idea how to punctuate a quote within a quote within a quote, since single and double quotes were the limits of his repertoire, but that also was another question for another day.

Unlike ninety-nine out of a hundred readers, Ruby immediately grasped these subtleties and was drawn further into them as she read. She was capable of sitting silently in front of one sentence for an hour or more, watching the kaleidoscopic patterns of meaning unfold.

Perhaps she was the only one of his readers who really understood.

APPENDIX B

<u>Regarding the First Publication of This Book
as *The Life and Times of Halycon Sage*,
Effects Thereof and Reactions Thereto</u>

(Removed from the Main Text by the Squid and
Designated as Badinage.)

Halycon Sage was wallowing in self-pity over in the darkest corner of the Canis Fidelis Grill and Juice Bar (formerly the Dirty Dog Bar). It was a good thing there was no more alcohol, neither here nor anywhere else, or he might have been tempted.

The cause of his sad swamp of self-pity was the fact that pretty much nobody had read his autobiography. After all the hell he had been through to write it, putting the best of his genius into something that went on for pages and pages and pages! His forehead broke out in a sweat just thinking about it.

Even his best friends, with all their encouragement and good intentions, were just too busy hunting, canning vegetables, setting up the new drip system for watering, and on and on in a boring litany of excuses. He suspected that even Preisczech had not read the thing, though Sage had typed out several copies on the old Smith-Corona and lovingly decorated the capitals that began the chapters. Of course Preisczech's English was quirky and variable—it was even remotely possible that he did not *read* the language.

Sage turned from contemplating the problem to deciding what to do about it. The problem was the title. The title was stupid. Who would want to read a book called *The Life and Times of Halycon Sage*?

It was long and boring and two thirds of the people who glanced at it would think his name was a misprint. Why, he wouldn't read it *himself* if he didn't know who he was! Well, he still didn't *quite* know who he was, but that touches on another topic too complex to address here.

So, a new title. *Horse!* thought Halycon Sage, *because his horse, No-Name Stupid, was a prominent character and featured on the cover.* He vaguely remembered plays in the late twentieth century with such titles, one word followed by an exclamation point. Punchy! People had wanted to see them; they had done well on Broadway. He was getting excited now. He could rename *One Hundred and One Cows: A Novel* and just call it *Cow!* It could be a series, a kind of farm animal theme. The third one would obviously be *Pig!* His enthusiasm deflated. No one would want to read *Pig!*

A short time later

Recognizing the knock on the door, the sudden flash of artistic genius, Halycon Sage leaped to his clattering old typewriter. For the few lonely readers possibly scattered across the post-Event deserts, forests, and mountains, and for the voluble critics who might one day people the bars and cafes of the future, he wrote his eighth Post-Modernist Minimalist Neo-Symbolist Pseudo-Realist novel, one more addition to the School of Literature that he had founded, and which had brought him worldwide fame while there was still a wide world to be famous in. The new book in its terse entirety read:

Hat!
I thought my hat had shrunk. But actually,
it was the wrong hat.
The End

Author's Note: The novel *Hat!* is based on an actual incident from the life of one Karima Vargas Bushnell, who memorably wore the wrong White Dervish Hat to *zikr* for weeks, railing against its newfound tightness, only to realize that the correctly fitted hat lay right beside it, in the same drawer, separated only by a loose tangle of scarves. The title *Hat!* was generated within a discussion among the minor intellectuals of her day (a.k.a., her family).

As of now there were only two serious readers in the known world (which was not very large). One was a critic, the other, an aspiring student of literature. Both responded quickly.

Basel Vasselschnauzer, formerly a noted New York literary critic, wrote:

> *Though the novel* Hat! *exemplifies the brevity, concision, and depth of insight we have come to expect from Mr. Sage—once again, he does not disappoint in any of these regards—this new work is obviously derivative. You will doubtless recognize the plot of* The Amazing Hat Mystery, *in which a tall, large-headed man and a short peanut-headed one inexplicably find that their hats, ordered from the most revered bespoke hatter to the crème de la crème, are suddenly and inexplicably too small in one case and too large in the other.*
>
> *The gentlemen's fiancés, neither of whom wish to walk down the aisle as a laughingstock, break off their respective engagements. (Or perhaps decline the men's proposals. The unfortunate conditions in this one-horse town since The Event prevent me from consulting a copy.)*
>
> *At the thrilling conclusion . . .*

[**Editor's Note**: Basel Vasselschnauzer has reacted to the dearth of serious new post-apocalypse literature by diving into romance novels, which behavior has doubtless affected his style.]

I say, at the thrilling conclusion, both hats are suddenly revealed to fit perfectly. While the Crumpet or Muffin or Egg, or whatever godforsaken anthropomorphic character is recounting this story at a London gentleman's club, attributes the mystery to 'something to do with the fourth dimension,' another character suggests that the hats were merely switched and then switched back again. Their listeners agree that this explanation is too far-fetched to bear consideration and that the fourth dimensional explanation is more likely.

I rest my case!

Not very admirable, Mr. Sage, not very admirable. A clear-cut case of plagiarism! (At least this title is better, though. No one would want to read a novel called The Life and Times of Halycon Sage.*)*

Your faithful reporter, editor, and everything else of that nature must recount here Halycon Sage's reply, delivered verbally over his shoulder from a galloping horse.

"I never heard of *The Amazing Hat Mystery*! Or of P.G. Wodehouse, either!" Which reply delivers him, guilty as charged, into the critic's hands and shows that even the revered Halycon Sage, beacon of truth, goodness, and integrity that he is, does have his little failings. For Basel Vasselschnauzer had not *mentioned* P.G. Wodehouse.

The second serious reader, Sophie McGregor, a brilliant young student and aspiring academic before The Event, wrote in her first draft:

We intend to base this analysis on the novel alone, along with its title. We may safely ignore the Author's Note, which many signs and markings familiar to critical scholars and wielders of textual analysis will agree is a spurious and later interpolation, perhaps written by some person seeking to bolster his or her importance (naming no names, Mr. B. V., Ph.D. so called).

The title, Hat! *is a distinct improvement over that of Mr. Sage's original first novel. It is short, punchy, to the point, and arouses interest. Certainly almost no one would wish to read something called* The Life and Times of Halycon Sage, *a title which may account for its paucity of readers, despite the unequalled brilliance that breathes beneath its covers.*

[**Editor's Note**: *Sophie too had been dipping into the stack of execrably written romances in the back of the Dirty Dog Bar. It is well known that authors' writing styles are influenced by what they read, and possibly one of them contained a line about someone or more than one person breathing beneath the covers.*]

Of the novel itself, much could be said. As usual with Mr. Sage's work, there are many layers to be mined and explored: There are practical, personal, individual, cultural, psychological, sociological, religious, and metaphysical implications. The absurd restrictions put on the length of literary analysis by Some Person styling herself 'the Editor,' publisher of a dinky village newspaper, makes it incumbent upon me to address only the veriest surface of these here.

As usual, in dealing with Mr. Sage's novels, we begin by quoting the entire literary production (minus the spurious Endnote). The extreme brevity of Sage's opi . . . opie . . . (note to self: look up plural of opus) allows the sincere student of literature this luxury.

Hat!
I thought my hat had shrunk.
But actually, it was the wrong hat.
The End

The novel consists of two sentences. The first speaks boldly, with a perception almost cinematic in its completeness, its all-roundedness, its profundity. The unnamed narrator, speaking either from a first person or an omniscient author perspective, simply states the phenomenon that has occurred and that constitutes the entire action of the book. (The second sentence consists of analysis, conclusion, and a tightly constructed summarizing of the philosophical implications.)

'I' indicates this mysterious narrator/author, either trapped within his/her/their individual mental bubble or observing the action broadly from above. Which of these is never revealed; we are left to guess, discuss, and ponder.

Second word: 'thought.' How much can be contained in one word, one single-syllabled verb! The entire corpus of individual cognition and cogitation, past tense, is captured here, with the brevity and terseness for which Mr. Sage is so justly revered.

'My hat.' The title concept, or object, introduces the element of the concrete, the physical world, in which all truly great literature must be grounded. That the hat is attributed to, claimed by, as belonging to, an undefined and amorphous 'I', merely rounds out the picture, adding the specificity that is also a hallmark of great literature. If 'I' and 'my' speak of the

individual, the personal and the inner, 'hat' is a metaphor for the entire physical universe.

The verb 'had' is grounded firmly in the past—not the simple past of 'has,' which might be used in any casual conversation, but the deep, rooted past of 'had.' Who knows, who can dare to guess, how long ago this storied past was set in? And whence?

'Shrunk.' What a world of disappointment, of unmet expectations, of glorious and far-ranging dreams belied, denied, and devastated, lies in this simple word. That which was great is great no more! That which strode out with high hopes in the morning of the world, now slinks back, ignominious, ashamed and self-conscious, for tea and muffins.

If only the neighbors don't see! If only no one remembers! That which promised so much, setting off to the blare of trumpets and the waving of purple flags and pennants, riding swift horses, sure to conquer the world and the hearts of men and women, returns home now, ragged, careworn, and dust covered. How much shame and pain are contained in that one word: shrunk!

'But actually, it was the wrong hat.' How much is contained here as well, all the comedy and tragedy of Shakespearean confusion between male and female identical twins, messages gone

329

awry, star-crossed lovers. I find that intellectual weariness and the necessity of pickling

"Yes, ALRIGHT, I'm coming!"

compel me to put off analysis of the seminal second sentence till another day.
To be continued . . .

APPENDIX C

<u>Halycon Sage's *Forget About it Trilogy* (or *Dinosaur Trilogy)* with Brief Introduction</u>

The next three pages contain Sage's remarkable *Dinosaur Trilogy*. Since he could never decide whether to call it *The Dinosaur Trilogy* or *The Forget about It Trilogy* or, indeed, whether to capitalize the A in about—we are including both titles.

The concluding novel is the best known example of the hard-boiled branch of the Post-Modernist Minimalist Neo-Symbolist Pseudo-Realist School of Literature founded by Halycon Sage. We leave you now to the contemplation of creation, time, and dinosaurs.

The Land Before Time Forgot Itself
by Halycon Sage

After Creator thought up the world, He let it develop through Evolution. Of course, He was always hands-on, in touch with every being at every moment, though not all of them knew it.

He made Time and Space like someone stretching a rubber band into a square on their thumbs and forefingers.

He gave Evolution some autonomy so it wouldn't be bored.

Space stretched out and sunned itself.

Evolution was having a party with microbes and sea life. Reaching the peak of its ambitions, it made huge, snaky-necked things and things with giant teeth.

It intended to give them Intelligence, Telepathy, and Thumbs.

At this point, Time became jealous, and conspired with Space (now irritable from sunburn) to make some little monkeys out of mud.

Those crazy monkeys took over everything!!!

The dinosaurs, in utter disgust, shrunk down to birds and flew away.

Of course, Creator knew about this from always— not being stuck in the linear timestream.

It was all part of the Plan, including the monkeys and what they turned into, and Preisczech and the Nanobots, and also *you*, who are reading this right now.

The End

The Land the Dinosaurs Forgot
by Halycon Sage

For quite a while after Creator made Evolution and told it to go do stuff, the dinosaurs were having a wonderful time! But when the little monkeys made of mud showed up and ruined everything, they shrank down to birds and flew away.

Several former dinosaurs sat disconsolately on a branch. It was raining.

"This sucks!" said one.

"Oh, go eat a worm," said another.

To think that they had once been kings of the forest, queens of the planet, watching their thumbs slowly evolve on their tiny claws, looking forward to playing chess!

"Hmmmm," said one.

"What's that?" asked another one. "Speak up, I can't hear you, you're just making a funny noise."

"Hmmm mmmm eeeet wh-yewww," said the first one.

"Chuck-a-WEE! Chuck-a-WEE!," said another, catching on.

"You guys are nuts!" said the first one, turning away.

The End

Forget about It
by Halycon Sage

Third in the *Forget About It* Trilogy

From the Hard-boiled Division
of the Post-Modernist Minimalist
Neo-Symbolist Pseudo-Realist
School of Literature

Chapter One

They say there ain't no dinosaurs no more, but they're wrong. There's a whole dinosaur underground the average citizen ain't aware of.

How do I know this? Because dinosaurs are my business. I track 'em. They call me Tracker Don. Get it? Get it? Tracker Don (a Trachodon).

Chapter Two

They say it takes one to know one. Well, they're right because I *am* one, and I know a *bunch* of 'em. There's Terry Don—a high-flyin' dinosaur dame you shouldn't oughta turn your back on. And there's Iguana Don. He might be a plant eater, but he's connected, and if you see him comin', you better get lost real fast and make like you ain't seen nothin'. And I'm just getting started.

They say the Dons are bad—you've all heard of Mafia Dons—but they don't scare me, maybe because they're family. The Saurs are a lot worse. Because, Buddy, when they get *saur*, ain't nobody happy! Get it? Get it?

—Tracker Don, Dinosaur Detective

Chapter Three

One day, Tracker Don, Dinosaur Detective, was meeting with a snitch out behind the Dirty Dog Bar. The guy was a runty little Stegoceras[1], barely 6.5 feet. He might be little, but this snitch had enough dope[2] to blow the whole Saurus ring sky high.

He was spilling the beans like they was jellybeans, when suddenly he stopped dead. There was a couple of iguanodons just ducking out of the alley.

He turned pale green.

"Oh my God!" he exclaimed. "I think they *saur* us!" Get it? Get it?

---

1. No, *not* Stegosaurus. But the confusion over names might be the root of his low status and self-esteem. —Basel Vasselschnauzer, editor
2. No, not drugs, you idiot. Information! —B.V.[3]
3. Basel! Manners, please —Unidentified Speaker

"Sage, what are you doing out there? We've got committee meetings!"

"Coming, Ruby."

And the sensitive author crunched up the pages of his terrible, terrible new novel into a big ball and launched it into the wastebasket, where it landed with a satisfying thud.

"Fuhgeddaboudit," mumbled Halycon Sage.

The End

END NOTES

1 *Something Wicked This Way Comes.*

2 Grok, from *Stranger in a Strange Land*, by Robert Heinlein. To understand something deeply. Literally means "to drink".

3 Edgar Rice Burroughs, author of the Tarzan books, and an actor who played the character in 12 films beginning in 1932.

4 George Sand, the pen name of Aurore Dupin, popular French novelist of the European Romantic Period.

5 Nancy Farmer's *The Ear, the Eye and the Arm* introduces the idea of a mirrored wall enclosing a protected area.

6 *Foundation*, Isaac Asimov.

7 *Habibi, umi, subhanallah.* Common Arabic words meaning "My beloved," "Mommy" or "my mom," and "Glory be to God".

8 Kilgore Trout, Kurt Vonnegut's imaginary author.

9 Jenny Jenny (867-5309)," a song released in 1981.

10 *Tarzan, Zorro, The Prisoner of Zenda,* and *The Lone Ranger.* The original novel *The Mark of Zorro* is far better than the countless shows and movies it spawned; *The Prisoner of Zenda* is now largely forgotten. Two delicious treats for lovers of high romantic adventure.

11 William Blake, an exalted visionary, poet, painter, and printmaker of the Romantic Period.

12 *The Way Beyond* is considered by some authorities to be merely Part One of the multi-part series The Sage Chronicles.

13 The Squids' luminescence. In a fifty years or so, if the new civilization lasts that long, Earth scientists will discover that the Squidren are lighted in much the same way as the phosphorescent creatures of Earth's deep seas and for much the same reasons.

14 *The Fellowship of the Ring*, J.R.R. Tolkien.

15 *Steppenwolf*, Herman Hesse. A metaphysical and psychological novel of great depth. If I had to pick a favorite book (impossible task!), it just might be this one.

16 *God's Smuggler* by Brother Andrew.

17 From the *Wird Sharif Kabir* (Greater, or Morning, Litany) of Pir Nureddin Jerrahi, a Sufi saint and the founder of a mystical lineage.

18   *Granfaloon,* from Kurt Vonnegut's novel *Cat's Cradle* (noun). A group of two or by Vonnegut was "people named Smith."

19   "Stomachs." Since they don't eat, the Squidren do not have actual stomachs. The organs mentioned are their equivalent, used for digesting light, sound, and other vibrations.

20   The imaginary book *Novel* and its imaginary author were inspired by real life author Robert Grudin and his novel, *Book.* There's more about this in the Afterword, but you should know that *Book* contains a "Rebellion of the Footnotes," which is quite hilarious.

21   Guys, dudes, people. From *Hitchhiker's Guide to the Galaxy.*

22   *Pride and Prejudice,* Jane Austin. The classic romantic novel of manners: origin, along with the work of the Brontes, of many conventions of the modern romance novel. (The writing style takes some getting used to for the modern reader. If you have a silly sense of humor, you might enjoy the movie *Lost in Austen,* in which a young woman obsessed with this book travels into and out of it through a portal behind her bathtub).

23   The machine that woke the Nanobots is a real, physical object located on True Earth. You can view it here: https://karimavargasbushnell.com/what-red-button/

24   *The Lion, the Witch and the Wardrobe,* C.S. Lewis. In *The Chronicles of Narnia,* four children first enter another dimension through the back of an old wardrobe.

25   *West Side Story,* musical production and movie about a modern Romeo and Juliet caught between rival street gangs in New York City.

26   This sentence mirrors the rather weak and pointless-seeming title of Sage's second novel, *Everything in the Universe is Fine Right Now,* indicating that the author may already have been traveling between times and dimensions at the beginning of Book One.

27   In a further indication that the Squidiler were upset beyond all measure, this communication did not use the now-familiar fiery letters. From this point on, the Squid use or do not use these letters at will depending upon the content. For it is a well-known principle of the Squidish language that the font must serve the text, rather than vice versa.

28   *The Wind in the Willows.* Like so many children's books (e.g., the Mary Poppins and Pooh books), the written version is more nuanced and interesting than any movie or TV adaptation.

29   "The Adventure of the Blanched Soldier," one of 12 stories in *The Casebook of Sherlock Holmes.* As with most Sherlock Holmes stories, this is well worth reading.

30   Squid Coloration: The males shade from blue to peacock green except in times of extreme stress when they, like the females, shade to purple. The zi genders are blue tinged with magenta, and the magenta becomes deeper and richer in moments of emotional engagement. While they are quite beautiful, the Squidren as a whole have an unaccountable prejudice against their color.

31   Unpublished poem asserting "All is Light," by American Sufi author, poet, and spiritual teacher, who practiced and held membership in several religious traditions.

32   *The Qur'an* — The holy book of Islam.